Emily Brontë

Wuthering Heights

咆哮山莊

Illustrated by Gianluca Folì

The Commercial Press

Contents 目錄

故事錄音開始和結束的標記　start ▶ stop ■

MAIN CHARACTERS

Catherine Earnshaw

Edgar Linton

Cathy Linton

Hindley Earnshaw

Hareton Earnshaw

Heathcliff

Isabella Linton

Linton Heathcliff

Vocabulary

1 Read the following description of the area around the Brontë's home village of Haworth, in West Yorkshire. Match the words with their correct definitions below. Use a dictionary to help you where necessary.

Brontë Country is an area in West Yorkshire. It is a windswept land of hills, purple-flowered heather and wild moors. It is the inspiration for this classic novel by Emily Brontë. The geology in Brontë Country is mostly a dark sandstone which makes the crags and scenery here appear bleak and desolate. Up in the high moors, small torrents and waterfalls race down into green wooded valleys, past fields of sheep and small trees, which have been shaped and bent by the wind.

1 ☐ windswept	**a**	empty and cold
2 ☐ heather	**b**	type of sedimentary rock
3 ☐ wild	**c**	low, evergreen plant, with small flowers
4 ☐ moors	**d**	windy
5 ☐ sandstone	**e**	steep or vertical rocks
6 ☐ crags	**f**	deserted, abandoned
7 ☐ bleak	**g**	uninhabited, uncultivated
8 ☐ desolate	**h**	open land with few trees

2 Match the job or title to the correct definition.

1 ☐ tenant	**a**	person paid to work in someone's house
2 ☐ landlord	**b**	a man's legally married female partner
3 ☐ servant	**c**	person who pays rent
4 ☐ housekeeper	**d**	(*old fashioned*) man with authority in a house
5 ☐ wife		
6 ☐ daughter-in-law	**e**	owner of rented property
	f	(*old fashioned*) woman with authority in a house
7 ☐ Master		
8 ☐ Mistress	**g**	a woman paid to run a house
	h	woman married to a person's son

Writing and Grammar

3 Read the following paragraph from the first chapter of the book, then fill in the gaps, using the correct verb in the correct tense or form.

> to describe • to be well named • to be • to (not) grow •
> to hear • to lean • to moan • to roar • to escape

Wuthering Heights **(1)** _____ the name of Mr Heathcliff's dark house, and it **(2)** _____, I am sure. 'Wuthering' is a word they use here in the north of England **(3)** _____ the sound of the wind as it **(4)** _____ across these high moors. Indeed, the few pine trees around the house were short and **(5)** _____ straight, but **(6)** _____ over as if **(7)** _____ the wind. On this bright spring day, I almost **(8)** _____ the wind **(9)** _____ through the house and into the hearts of its inhabitants.

Speaking

4 Discuss the following in pairs. Would you like to live in Wuthering Heights? Why? Why not? Use the ideas in the box below to help you.

old house	→ modern house	neighbours	→ isolated
		noisy	→ quiet
farmhouse	→ block of flats	warm and cosy	→ big rooms
city	→ countryside	full of character	→ practical
warm climate	→ cool climate		

5 Imagine you are arriving at an isolated farmhouse for the first time. Discuss the following questions in pairs.

- How would you feel if the people you met there did not look pleased to see you?
- How would you feel if the people you met were rude to you?
- How would you feel if you saw a ghost in the house?

Chapter One

'Let me in! Let me in!'

▶ 2 As I rode up to the grey, stone house, my heart warmed towards the man in his forties that I saw standing before me, his black eyes watching me suspiciously. I felt sure we would be friends.

'Mr Heathcliff?' I asked.

The man nodded.

'Mr Lockwood, sir, your new tenant at Thrushcross Grange.'

Mr Heathcliff nodded again, and through his teeth said, 'Come in.'

His words sounded more like 'go away' than an invitation to enter his farmhouse, which sat solid and low against the hillside.

'Joseph, take Mr Lockwood's horse,' he said.

The thin servant who appeared had an expression that would make vinegar taste sweet in comparison.

'The Lord help us!' he muttered[1], as he led my horse to the stable.

Wuthering Heights is the name of Mr Heathcliff's dark house, and it is well named, I am sure. 'Wuthering' is a word they use here in the north of England to describe the sound of the wind as it roars across these high moors[2]. Indeed, the few pine trees around the house were short and did not grow straight, but leant over as if to escape the wind. On this bright spring day, I almost heard the wind moaning through the house and into the hearts of its inhabitants.

1. **muttered:** 喃喃自語　　　　2. **moors:** 高沼

As I followed Mr Heathcliff, I saw, carved in stone above the door, 'Hareton Earnshaw' and the year '1500'.

The front door went straight into a great room full of dark furniture which looked as old as the house. I went to touch one of the dogs, but it snarled at me viciously[1]. Mr Heathcliff and I did not exchange many words, and after a few minutes I got up to go, promising him that I would come to see him the next day. His face did not show any enthusiasm for my next visit, but I was curious to get to know this man, so withdrawn[2] from the world.

The next day, the weather was bad. I had decided to stay at home, but the servants had not lit the fires and it was cold at Thrushcross Grange, so I walked the four miles up to Wuthering Heights. The first snow was falling as I arrived. I knocked and banged on the door, but there was no answer. Eventually, the sour face of Joseph appeared from a barn.

'Master's busy, and the Missus won't let you in,' and with that, he disappeared.

It began to snow heavily, and still no one opened the door. Then, through the snow I saw a young farm worker. He did not speak, but took me to the back of the house, through the kitchen, and into the big room I had seen the day before.

A fire burned in the huge fireplace, and a meal was set on the table. Sitting in a chair near the fire was a beautiful young woman. She did not move as I entered and did not speak, but stared at me with a coldness that matched the weather.

'Mrs Heathcliff?' I asked, but she did not answer. Trying to start a

1. **viciously:** 兇惡地   2. **withdrawn:** 孤僻

conversation, I said how pretty were the kittens I saw in a corner of the room.

'Strange choice of pet,' she said, unpleasantly.

When I looked more closely, I realised my mistake. They were not kittens but a pile of dead rabbits that the dogs had caught. The girl did not speak again, and we sat in complete silence for many minutes, until Mr Heathcliff and the young man who had shown me into the house, came in.

'I have kept my promise,' I said to my landlord, relieved[1] to break the silence.

'You should not have come up here in such weather,' was his answer. 'Do you know that you could get lost out here? Even people who know these moors well cannot find their way on evenings like this.'

'Perhaps one of your servants could guide me home?' I said.

'There is no one to take you,' he said. Then he turned to the young lady and demanded[2], 'Are you going to make the tea?'

'Is he to have any?' she asked, looking at me.

'Get it ready, will you?' He said this so aggressively that I was shocked. The way he spoke to the young lady was truly terrible. I no longer thought of Mr Heathcliff as a friend.

When the meal was ready, he invited me to join them, but no one spoke and I was not hungry.

'Your wife keeps a good house, Mr Heathcliff,' I said.

'My wife?' he said, with a look that seemed to come straight from the devil. 'Where is *she*, then?'

I realised my mistake: the young lady must be married to the young farm worker who sat eating in silence beside me.

---

1. **relieved:** 鬆一口氣　　　　　　2. **demanded:** 強烈要求

'Mrs Heathcliff is my daughter-in-law,' explained Heathcliff. As he spoke, he looked at her with intense hatred.

'Then you are the lucky man,' I said to the young man, but he looked as though I had hit him, turning bright red and clenching his fists in anger.

'Wrong again,' said Heathcliff with a smile, 'her husband is dead. I said she was my daughter-in-law,' he continued, 'therefore she must have married my son.'

'So this young man is...'

'Not my son.' Heathcliff smiled again, as if the idea of Hareton being his son was a good joke.

'My name is Hareton Earnshaw,' growled the young man, 'and I will teach you to respect it.'

I looked down quickly, not wanting to anger him further. We finished our meal, and I got up to look out of the window. The snow was falling thicker than ever, covering everything.

'It will be impossible for me to get home without a guide,' I said, but when I turned round, only Mrs Heathcliff was left in the room, with the servant, Joseph, coming in with food for the dogs.

'I don't know how you can stand there doing nothing,' said Joseph, his face pinched[1] and mean, his Yorkshire accent so strong I could hardly understand him. He was speaking to the young lady. 'You are useless, and you will never get any better. You will go to the devil like your mother before you.'

'You disgusting old hypocrite,' she replied. 'Aren't you afraid that the devil will come and take your soul[2]? In fact, I might ask him to do it for me as a special favour. I have been learning my spells! You don't think that red cow died by herself, do you?' and she looked at him as if she really were a witch.

---

1. **pinched:** 消瘦的，多形容臉   2. **soul:** 靈魂

Joseph was shocked, 'Oh, you are wicked, wicked. May the Lord save us from your evil ways.'

And with that he put down the dogs' food and left as quickly as he could. I thought that she was joking, but when I asked her to tell me the best way to get home in all this snow, she sat down in a chair with a candle and said rudely, 'Go back the way you came,' and opened her book.

'I see you will not help me, and since there is no one to guide me, I will have to stay here for the night.'

'You will have to ask *him*,' she said.

I heard a movement from the kitchen. 'Let this be a lesson to you to go walking on the moors in such weather,' said Heathcliff coming into the room. 'We do not have a room for guests, you will have to share with Hareton or Joseph.'

The thought did not appeal[1] to me.

'I will sleep here on a chair,' I said.

'No you won't. I will not have strangers wandering around the house while I sleep.'

With this final insult, I took my coat and went out into the night, almost running into Hareton.

'I'll go with him as far as the road to the Grange,' he said.

'You'll go with him to hell,' roared[2] Heathcliff. 'You still have the horses to look after.' And with that he left.

'A man's life is more important than the horses for one night,' said the young Mrs Heathcliff with more kindness than I expected. 'You must go, Hareton.'

'*You* will not command *me*,' snarled the young man.

'Then I hope his ghost will haunt you, and Mr Heathcliff never finds another tenant until the Grange is a ruin,' she answered sharply.

---

1. appeal: 吸引 ▶FCE◀   2. roared: 咆哮

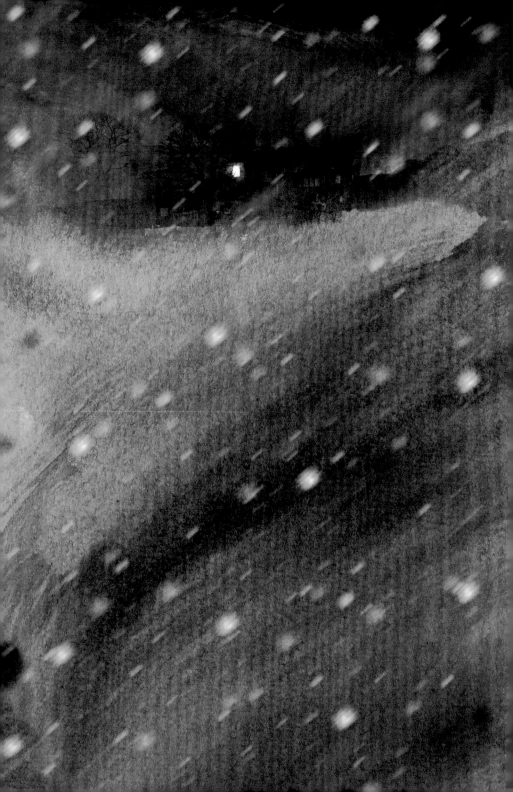

Joseph, hearing all the noise, came up with a lantern in his hand. Seeing my chance to escape, I snatched it from him and set off.

'Hey! Master, he's stealing the lantern,' shouted the ancient servant, calling the dogs. At that moment, two hairy monsters ran out, jumping up at my throat and knocking me over.

The lantern went out, but the dogs did not tear me to pieces as I expected, they started to lick me. I heard a guffaw[1] from both Heathcliff and Hareton. My nose had started bleeding badly and still Heathcliff laughed without coming over to help me. Fortunately, at that moment, the housekeeper came running out of the house.

'Are we murdering people on our doorstep now?' she said to Hareton. Then seeing how my nose bled, she said, 'I know a way to cure that,' and tipped a bucket of icy water down my neck.

At that point, Heathcliff stopped laughing, his face returning to its normal darkness, and he went off down the farmyard, while the woman, who told me her name was Zillah, led me shaking back into the house.

In the kitchen, she gave me a glass of brandy, and told me how sorry she was for all that had happened, then she handed me a candle and told me to follow her upstairs without making a sound.

'The master does not like anyone to use this room,' she said, but when I asked why, she said she had only been here a year or two; she did not know, and it was not a good idea to ask questions in this house.

❖ ❖ ❖

I said goodnight to her and got into the bed which was against a window. I put my candle on the window ledge[2] and saw that some words had been scratched into the wood. I looked more closely and read a name, repeated again and again, in letters large and small. *Catherine Earnshaw,*

---

1. **guffaw:** 大笑   2. **ledge:** 窗台、窗沿

then occasionally, *Catherine Heathcliff* and *Catherine Linton*. I read the names over and over until the letters were swimming in front of my eyes, and the *Catherines* were flying around my head like ghosts.

On the ledge were some old books. I opened one. Inside it was written *'Catherine Earnshaw – her book'*. In each of the books were written the same words, and what's more, someone had covered the margins of the books with small, neat writing. I moved the candle closer and began to read the faded words.

'An awful Sunday!' The words began. 'I wish my father were back. My brother Hindley is detestable[1], he is awful to Heathcliff. H and I are going to rebel. It was raining all day and we could not go to church, so H and I were sent upstairs to read our bibles with Joseph, while Hindley and Frances sat in front of the fire. Joseph kept us there for three hours, and when we came down, Hindley said, 'What, finished already?' When father was alive, we were allowed to play on Sundays; now if we make even the smallest sound, we are punished.

'You forget who is the master[2] here,' says the tyrant Hindley. 'Don't you dare put me in a bad mood. Frances, pull that boy's hair. I think he made a noise.'

She pulled it, then went to sit on her husband's knee, and they kissed and talked nonsense like two babies. We played quietly, but then Joseph came in.

'How can you play when the old master died only the other week? Read these Christian books and think about how to save your souls from the devil.' He gave us each a book, but I stood up and threw mine across the room, and H kicked his across the floor. Hindley came over and pushed us into the kitchen, while Joseph told us the devil would come and take our souls. We are going to run away.

---

1. **detestable:** 可憎   2. **master:** 主人

I imagine that Catherine and Heathcliff must have tried to run away, because the next section Catherine wrote said, 'I cannot believe how much Hindley has made me cry. My head aches with it. He has said that H is a vagabond[1] and is not to sit or eat with us any more. He blames[2] our father for being too kind to H. How could he say such a thing?'

As I read, my eyes began to feel heavy. I fell asleep and had a terrible nightmare. In it, I was trying to walk home in the snow, and Joseph was talking and talking, telling me to 'save my soul', repeatedly hitting a bible with his hand. When I woke, I saw it was still snowing. There was a pine tree outside the window, and there was a strong wind. The noise in my dream must have been a branch hitting the window, I decided, and went back to sleep.

I woke a second time. It was still night, and the branch was still knocking at the window. I opened the window to break the branch off, but when I reached my arm out, my fingers closed on the fingers of an ice-cold hand. I tried desperately to free my hand, but whatever held me was too strong. Then I heard a sad, little voice.

'Let me in! Let me in!' it said.

'Who are you?' I asked, still trying to free myself.

'Catherine Linton,' the voice replied, shivering with cold. 'I come home. I'd lost my way on the moors.'

As it spoke, I thought I saw a child's face through the window. I was terrified.

'Let me in!' the child cried again, 'It's been twenty years. I've been waiting twenty years.'

I freed my hand and shouting in fright, shut the window, piling the books in front of it. All the time the creature wailed, and the pile of books began to move in towards me.

---

1. vagabond: 流浪者、無業遊民

2. blames: 責怪 ▶FCE◀

I should not have shouted out in that way, because I soon heard footsteps coming towards my door. I lay back in my bed without making a sound.

'Is anyone there?' a man whispered. It was Heathcliff.

He stood in the door, holding a candle which was dripping down over his hand, his face as white as the wall behind him. I decided to tell him it was me and sat up in my bed. The effect on him was like an electric shock, the candle flew from his hand, and he was shaking so much he could hardly pick it up again.

'This place is full of ghosts,' I said.

'What do you mean?' he said. 'Go back to sleep, and for God's sake[1] do not shout like that again unless you are being murdered.'

'Well,' I answered, 'if that little monster Catherine Linton had got in, she probably would have killed me.'

'What can you mean by talking to me in this way?' he thundered[2]. 'How dare you!'

'I cannot sleep here, sir.'

Heathcliff took a minute to calm himself, then came into the room, 'Then you must finish the night in my room.'

I got up to leave, but as I went through the door, I heard Heathcliff burst into uncontrollable tears. He pushed the books out of the way and opened the window.

'Come in! Come in!' he sobbed. 'Oh, do come again, my heart's darling. Catherine, hear me this time.'

This ghost was cruel, as they often are, and she did not come back. I felt guilty that I had witnessed the distress of this troubled man and left silently. Long after I had walked down to the kitchen to warm myself by the fire, I could hear him quietly calling and sobbing into the empty darkness of the night.

---

1. for God's sake: 看在上帝的份上   2. thundered: 怒吼

FCE - Reading Comprehension

1 **Choose the best answer – A, B, C or D**

1 When does the story start?
A ☐ Spring.
B ☐ Summer.
C ☐ Autumn.
D ☐ Winter.

2 How does Mr Lockwood arrive at the house the second time?
A ☐ On foot.
B ☐ On horseback.
C ☐ In a carriage.
D ☐ On a bicycle.

3 How is Mr Lockwood greeted by the people at the house?
A ☐ Warmly.
B ☐ Kindly.
C ☐ Aggressively.
D ☐ Sadly.

4 How would you describe Mr Lockwood?
A ☐ Selfish.
B ☐ Naive.
C ☐ Aggressive.
D ☐ Generous.

5 How would you describe Heathcliff?
A ☐ Polite.
B ☐ Shy.
C ☐ Angry.
D ☐ Friendly.

6 What is Mr Lockwood's reaction to seeing the ghost?
A ☐ He is very upset and starts crying.
B ☐ He is curious to find out more about her.
C ☐ He is calm and wants to speak to her.
D ☐ He is frightened and angry.

Reading Comprehension

2 **Match the names of the characters we meet in Chapter One with their job or relationship to each other.**

1 ☐ Heathcliff   **a** widow of Heathcliff's son
2 ☐ Mr Lockwood   **b** male servant at Wuthering Heights
3 ☐ Catherine   **c** owner of Wuthering Heights
4 ☐ Hareton   and Thrushcross Grange
5 ☐ Joseph   **d** Heathcliff's tenant at Thrushcross Grange
6 ☐ Zillah   **e** the ghost of the woman Heathcliff loved
7 ☐ Cathy/   **f** housekeeper at Wuthering Heights
     Catherine   **g** young man who works on the farm
     Linton

Vocabulary

3a **Use the following verbs, describing the way someone said something, to fill in the gaps. Remember to use the correct form of the verb.**

> cry • laugh • shout • snarl •
> sob • talk • thunder • wail • whisper

1 'You will not command me,' _____ the young man.
2 'Hey! Master, he's stealing the lantern,' _____ the ancient servant.
3 My nose had started bleeding badly and still Heathcliff _____.
4 They kissed and _____ nonsense like two babies.
5 'Let me in!' the child _____ again.
6 All the time the creature _____.
7 'Is anyone there?' a man _____.
8 'What can you mean by talking to me in this way?' he _____.
9 'Come in! Come in!' he _____.

3b Now put the verbs from exercise 3a under the correct heading below. This will help you put them into groups of similar meaning.

unhappy	angry	happy	speak normally

Word-building

4a Complete the table using nouns and adverbs from Chapter 1.

noun	adverb
	aggressively
	desperately
repeated	
sharp	
suspicious	
unpleasant	
	rudely
	viciously

4b Fill in the gaps with the correct adverb from exercise 4a.

1 ... his black eyes watching me _____.

2 ... it snarled at me _____.

3 'Strange choice of pet,' she said, _____.

4 He said this so _____ that I was shocked.

5 ... she sat down [...] and said _____, "Go back the way you came."

6 'Then I hope his ghost will haunt you [...],' she answered _____.

7 Joseph was talking and [...] _____ hitting a bible...

8 I tried _____ to free my hand.

FCE – Grammar

5 **Read this imaginary description of events written by Mr Lockwood, then fill in the gaps with the correct preposition.**

I rode **(1)** _____ to Wuthering Heights **(2)** _____ a fine, spring day. It was a low, solid house, built **(3)** _____ dark stone. A man was standing **(4)** _____ the gate. He looked **(5)** _____ me suspiciously, but I introduced myself. He told me his name was Heathcliff. He called a servant to take my horse, and **(6)** _____ he took it to the stable, he seemed angry. Heathcliff invited me **(7)** _____ the house. The big room we entered was filled with dark, old furniture, **(8)** _____ old as the house itself, and there was a fire burning in the huge fireplace at one end of the room.

PRE-READING ACTIVITIES

Listening

▶ 3 **6 a** **Listen to the beginning of Chapter Two. Are these statements true (T) or false (F)?**

		T	F
1	Mr Lockwood returns home in the evening.	☐	☐
2	He feels depressed and sits doing nothing all day.	☐	☐
3	The housekeeper comes in with the dinner.	☐	☐
4	Mr Lockwood decides to talk to her to cheer himself up.	☐	☐
5	Heathcliff doesn't live at Thrushcross Grange because he's very poor.	☐	☐
6	Catherine is married to Heathcliff's cousin.	☐	☐
7	Catherine was a Linton before she married.	☐	☐
8	Heathcliff's son is Catherine's cousin.	☐	☐

6 b **Listen again and correct the false statements.**

Chapter Two

'Heathcliff, how black and cross you look!'

3 I returned home in the morning feeling depressed and sat doing nothing all day.

When the housekeeper at Thrushcross Grange, Nelly Dean, came in with my tea, I decided to talk to her to cheer myself up.

'How long have you been working here, Mrs Dean?' I asked.

'Eighteen years, sir. I came when the mistress[1] was married. When she died, the master kept me on as housekeeper.'

'Why does Mr Heathcliff not live here?' I asked. 'This house is so much better than that one up on the moors. Is he too poor to look after it?'

'Not at all, sir. He is as rich as can be, but he is very mean[2] about money.'

'He had a son, I believe.'

'Yes, married to my Miss Catherine who lives up at Wuthering Heights. She was a Linton before she married, my master's daughter. She grew up in this house.'

For a moment, I was confused. Catherine Linton? But of course, the young lady at Wuthering Heights was not the ghost I had seen the night before.

'She married her cousin, the son of Mr Heathcliff and my master's sister, Isabella Linton.'

1. mistress: 女主人　　　　　　　　2. mean: 吝嗇小氣

22

'And the other young man, Hareton Earnshaw?'

'He is her cousin too, sir. His father was the brother of the young lady's mother. How was the young lady when you saw her?'

'Very well and very pretty, but not very happy.'

'That does not surprise me,' she said, 'living up there with that Mr Heathcliff for company.'

'Yes, he is a difficult man,' I agreed. 'Nelly, tell me, what has happened in his life to make him so disagreeable?'

'I will tell you the story if you want, but first I must get my sewing[1].'

She came back with it, and sat down by the fire to tell me about the strange people I had met at Wuthering Heights.

I started working at Wuthering Heights when I was a girl, about thirty years ago. I was looking after the Earnshaws' children, Miss Cathy and Master Hindley. One day, old Mr Earnshaw said he had to go to Liverpool, and that he would bring the children back presents.

We waited for three days for him to return, and it was late on the evening of the third day, when the door was flung[2] open and in came Mr Earnshaw. He threw himself in a chair, laughing, saying how exhausted he was, and that he had found a present for all of us. He opened up his coat, and there, hiding beneath it was a dirty, ragged, black-haired child, and when he spoke, none of us could understand what language he was speaking. He looked about six years old, the same age as Miss Cathy.

Mrs Earnshaw was not happy to have another mouth to feed, but her husband explained he had found the child homeless and starving on the streets of Liverpool. He had not been able to find the child's family, so had brought him home.

---

1. **sewing:** 縫紉   2. **flung:** 猛扔

'We shall call him Heathcliff,' he said 'and he is to live with us from now on.'

Cathy and Heathcliff quickly became friends, but Hindley hated him, and to tell the truth, so did I.

We were constantly unkind to the dark child, but he never complained when Hindley hit him or I pushed him out of the way. Perhaps he was used to being treated like that.

He was a great favourite of Mr Earnshaw, and this made Hindley hate him even more. From the moment Heathcliff arrived, there was bad feeling in the house; but when the children all got the measles[1], Heathcliff was as patient as a lamb throughout his illness, and I became fond[2] of him.

As they grew up, Hindley continued to treat Heathcliff badly, and still he didn't complain. I thought this was because he had a forgiving character. You will see how wrong I was about that.

When Miss Cathy was thirteen years old, her father, Mr Earnshaw, became ill, and Joseph began to poison his mind against all the children. Hindley was sent away to college.

I hoped that with Hindley gone, there would be peace in the house, but I was wrong about that too. You have met Joseph?' she asked. I nodded.

'A horrible, poisonous man, sir. Every day he told Mr Earnshaw how bad Miss Cathy and Heathcliff were, but this only made Miss Cathy's behaviour even worse. Oh, she was a wild thing: she would try your patience all day with her bad ways. But you could not stay cross with her for long. At the end of the day, she would come to you chatting, laughing and singing as if nothing was wrong. Her big problem was that she was much too fond of Heathcliff. The worst punishment we could think of for Miss Cathy was to keep her separate from him.

❖ ❖ ❖

1. measles: 麻疹　　　　　　　　　　2. fond: 喜愛

One day she had been so naughty that when she asked her father to forgive her, he said, 'No, Cathy, I cannot love you. You are worse than your brother.'

The old man died not long after that, and Mr Hindley came home for the funeral. What amazed us, and set the neighbours gossiping[1] – he brought a wife with him. She was a silly thing, but harmless enough. She loved everything she saw in the house, but became very upset after Mr Earnshaw's funeral.

'Have those people gone away, Nelly? I hate seeing all those black clothes.'

When I asked her why, she said she was terrified of dying. I did not think her likely to die, though I did notice that she had difficulty breathing sometimes. At first, she was delighted to find a new sister in Cathy and would chat to her for hours, but she soon tired of her, and when she told Hindley how much she hated Heathcliff, he became a tyrant. Heathcliff was no longer allowed to sit and eat with the family, nor was he to have lessons. He was to be treated as a servant.

Heathcliff seemed to accept this. Miss Cathy taught him what she had learnt in her lessons, and worked or played with him in the fields.

The young master was so caught up in his wife that he did not care how Cathy and Heathcliff behaved or what they did. They were turning into little savages[2]. One of their biggest pleasures was running away to the moors in the morning and staying there all day. When they were punished for it, they simply laughed. As soon as they were together again, Miss Cathy would forget that she had been sent to bed without her supper; Heathcliff would not remember how he had been hit by Joseph too many times to count.

---

1. **gossiping:** 說三道四   2. **savages:** 沒有教養的人

One wet Sunday evening, they were sent out of the room for making a noise, but when I came to look for them to send them to bed, they were nowhere to be found.

We searched the whole house until late at night. Eventually, Master Hindley became furious, and told us to lock[1] all the doors and windows even if Cathy and Heathcliff had to stay out all night in the rain. I stayed up waiting, until eventually I heard footsteps in the yard and went out to see who it was.

There was Heathcliff, alone. I was terribly worried.

'Where is Miss Cathy?' I asked him. 'No accident, I hope?'

'She is at Thrushcross Grange,' he said, 'and I would have been there too, but they did not have the manners[2] to ask me to stay.'

'What in the world is she doing at Thrushcross Grange?' I asked as I took him into the kitchen to dry himself.

'Cathy and I were on the moors, when we saw the lights of Thrushcross Grange and decided to see how the Lintons spend their Sundays, to see if they are always sent out in the cold and punished like we are, while their mother and father sit eating and drinking, singing and laughing by the fire. Do you think that is how they spend their Sundays?'

'Probably not,' I answered, 'but I expect they are good children.'

'Good children?' he cried. 'We ran down to the Grange and looked in through the windows. Ah, everything in it was beautiful, and Mr and Mrs Linton weren't there, so Edgar and Isabella had the place to themselves. Cathy and I would have been in heaven, but what do you think your good children were doing, Nelly? Screaming and fighting over who would hold their pet dog!

How we laughed at them. Cathy or I would never be like that with

---

1. **lock:** 鎖上   2. **manners:** 風度、禮儀

each other. If you gave me a thousand lives, I would not want to live like they do.'

'Yes, but why is Miss Cathy not with you, Heathcliff?' I asked.

'The young Lintons heard us laughing and began shouting 'Mamma! Papa!' We ran away. I was pulling Cathy by the hand, but suddenly she fell down.

'Run, Heathcliff, run,' she said, 'They have let out a dog, and it has got me by the ankle!' I swore[1] and cursed, and tried to get the dog off Cathy's leg, but a servant came up, pulled the beast off and picked Cathy up; she was white with the pain. I followed them into the house, swearing and promising vengeance.

When they had Cathy in the light, Edgar Linton recognised her from church, 'That's Miss Earnshaw. Look how her ankle bleeds.'

They did not believe him at first.

'I cannot believe that Hindley allows his sister to run around so wild,' said Mr Linton, 'and who is she with? Isn't it that foreign brat[2] Mr Earnshaw picked up in Liverpool? This cannot be right.'

They told me I was a wicked boy, so I swore at them, and they threw me out, saying that they would tell Hindley of my behaviour. But how gentle they were with Cathy! When I looked in at the window, they had bandaged her foot and sat her in front of the fire. Isabella had given her some little cakes, which she was feeding to the dog, while a servant brushed her hair. She gave a spark of spirit to those vacant, blue eyes of the Lintons. They were full of stupid admiration for her; she is so superior to them – to everyone on earth, is she not, Nelly?'

'That's enough, now,' I said to him. 'When Mr Hindley hears of your behaviour, there will be consequences, you will see. You are incurable, Heathcliff.'

1. swore: 咒罵   2. brat: 頑童

I was not wrong. Heathcliff was not beaten, but he was told that if he ever spoke to Miss Cathy again, he would immediately be sent away. In the Lintons, Frances and Hindley had seen their chance to turn Miss Cathy into a young lady and get her away from Heathcliff.

Cathy stayed at Thrushcross Grange five weeks, till Christmas. By that time her ankle was cured, and her behaviour much improved. And when she returned, instead of a wild, hatless little savage jumping into the house and running over to squeeze¹ the life out of you with a hug², we saw a dignified little person riding a lovely black pony, her hair beautifully curled under her fur hat, and wearing a long, elegant coat.

'Why Cathy, you are quite a beauty!' Hindley said as he lifted her from the horse. 'I hardly recognised you – She looks like a lady, doesn't she, Frances?'

'She does,' replied his wife, 'but she must make sure she does not become wild again here. Nelly, come and help Miss Cathy take off her coat and hat; careful now, we do not want to disarrange that lovely hair.'

Her eyes sparkled when she saw the dogs come running to her, but she did not want to touch them in case they made her clothes dirty. She kissed me gently. I was covered in flour from making the Christmas cake, so she could not give me a hug; then she looked round for Heathcliff. Hindley and Frances watched anxiously to see if they had been successful in separating the two friends.

Heathcliff did not show himself at first. He had been uncared for before Miss Cathy went away, but while she was at the Grange, he had been completely neglected. I made him wash once a week, but his clothes were filthy from his work on the farm, his hair was

1. **squeeze:** 擠壓 ▶FCE◀　　　　2. **hug:** 擁抱

unbrushed, and his face and hands had not been washed for days. He hid behind a door, dark and scowling[1], watching this bright, graceful young lady, so different from the wild Cathy he had known only a few weeks before.

'Is Heathcliff not here?' she asked, pulling off her gloves to reveal hands which had become white from doing nothing and staying indoors.

'Heathcliff, come and greet[2] Miss Cathy like the other servants,' said Hindley, pleased to see him so uncomfortable.

Cathy saw him then. She ran to him, threw her arms round him and kissed his cheek seven or eight times, but then she stepped back, looked at him and laughed.

'Why, Heathcliff, how black and cross you look! But that's because I'm used to Edgar and Isabella Linton. Well, Heathcliff, have you forgotten me?'

Heathcliff did not speak.

'Shake hands, Heathcliff,' said Hindley.

'I shall not!' he replied. 'I shall not stand and be laughed at!'

'I did not mean to laugh at you,' said Miss Cathy, 'but you look so dirty and cross. If you wash your face and brush your hair, it will be better.'

'I shall be as dirty as I want to. I like to be dirty and I will be dirty.' Then he ran out of the room.

Later, I went to find Heathcliff in the stable.

'Come now, Heathcliff. I have some little cakes for you and Miss Cathy. There is no one in the kitchen. You can spend some time together on your own.'

But he did not come that evening or the next day, and Miss Cathy was very upset.

1. **scowling:** 怒目而視　　　2. **greet:** 打招呼

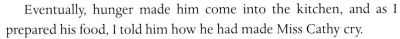

Eventually, hunger made him come into the kitchen, and as I prepared his food, I told him how he had made Miss Cathy cry.

'Well, I cried last night, too. And I had more reason to cry than she did.'

'The Lintons are coming today, if you put a smile on your face instead of sulking[1] and clean yourself up, maybe you can stay with them and Miss Cathy.'

He agreed eventually, and by the time the Lintons arrived, he looked very handsome. But seeing him, Edgar Linton said, 'What long hair he has! I am surprised he can see where he is going.'

Heathcliff was furious. He picked up a bowl of hot apple sauce from the table and threw it over Edgar's face and neck.

Hindley took Heathcliff by the collar and took him upstairs to beat[2] him, then locked him in his room. For the rest of the day, I was surprised to see Miss Cathy chatting and laughing as if nothing had happened, but when evening came, I saw her hide a tear. While the others were singing Christmas songs, she left the room without them noticing and brought Heathcliff into the kitchen. But he was so ill from being beaten by Hindley that he did not want to eat. Miss Cathy went back to her guests, and he sat by the fire with his chin in his hands. When I asked what he was thinking about, I was shocked by his reply.

'I am planning how to get my revenge on Hindley,' he said. 'I don't care how long it takes. I will do it. I only hope he does not die before I do! Don't be cross with me, Nelly. While I am thinking, I cannot feel the pain.'

---

1. sulking: 生悶氣   **2. beat:** 打、擊

Reading Comprehension

1 Answer the questions in complete sentences.

1 Who did Mr Lockwood hear Heathcliff's story from?

_____

2 Where did Heathcliff come from?

_____

3 Why did Mr Earnshaw bring him home?

_____

4 What was Heathcliff's relationship with Hindley when they were growing up?

_____

5 What was Heathcliff's relationship with Cathy?

_____

6 Why did Heathcliff and Cathy decide to look through the windows at Thrushcross Grange?

_____

7 What did they see?

_____

8 Why did Cathy stay at Thrushcross Grange?

_____

9 How had Cathy changed when she came back home?

_____

FCE – Writing

2 Chronicle. Write an article about Heathcliff's life, from childhood. Write 120-150 words.

Speaking

3 **Look at your article, and discuss the following questions in pairs.**

- Are there any similarities between the young and the older Heathcliff? What are they?
- Does Heathcliff's character get better or worse as he gets older?
- Do you feel sorry for the young Heathcliff?

Vocabulary

4a **Decide if the following adjectives have a generally positive or negative meaning, and write them under the correct columns.**

> cross • depressed • dirty • disagreeable • forgiving •
> harmless • horrible • mean • naughty • patient •
> poisonous • silly • unkind • wicked • wild

Positive	Negative

4b **Looking at the adjectives above, which adjectives can you use to describe...**

Joseph	_____
Frances	_____
Hindley	_____
Nelly	_____
Heathcliff	_____
Cathy	_____
Mr Lockwood	_____

Grammar

5 **Continuous and Simple tenses and gerunds. Put the verb in the correct form in the gaps below.**

1 I returned home in the morning _____ (feel) depressed and sat _____ (do) nothing all day.

2 The housekeeper at Thrushcross Grange, Nelly Dean, _____ (come) in with my tea.

3 I _____ (decide) to talk to her to cheer myself up.

4 'How long _____ (work) here, Mrs Dean?' I asked.

5 I started _____ (work) at Wuthering Heights when I was a girl.

6 I _____ (look) after the Earnshaws' children, Miss Cathy and Master Hindley.

7 Cathy and Heathcliff quickly became friends, but Hindley _____ (hate) him, and to tell the truth, so did I.

8 Perhaps he was used to _____ (treat) like that.

9 She _____ (give) a spark of spirit to those vacant, blue eyes of the Lintons.

10 'I _____ (plan) how to get my revenge on Hindley,' he said.

6 **Find fourteen phrasal verbs (verb + preposition) in the wordsearch below.**

S	L	A	U	G	H	E	D	A	T
E	T	S	A	T	D	O	W	N	L
N	I	K	E	P	T	O	N	S	I
T	R	G	R	E	W	U	P	T	V
O	E	K	E	E	P	T	O	A	E
U	D	C	A	M	E	I	N	Y	W
T	O	B	L	O	W	U	P	O	I
O	F	F	E	E	D	T	O	U	T
F	R	U	N	A	W	A	Y	T	H
C	A	U	G	H	T	U	P	I	N

Speaking

7 **Do you agree or disagree with the following statements? Discuss your answers in pairs.**

1 Mr Earnshaw was right to bring the boy home with him.
2 Hindley was right to be jealous of Heathcliff.
3 Hindley's treatment of Heathcliff is unjustifiable.
4 Heathcliff was patient and forgiving.
5 Cathy's transformation into a young lady is believable.
6 I feel sorry for Heathcliff.

Agree	Disagree	Don't know

PRE-READING ACTIVITIES

8 a **Before you listen to Chapter Three, read the following statements. Do you think they will be true (T) or false (F)?**

T F

1 Hindley and Frances have a son called Hareton. ☐ ☐
2 Frances dies. ☐ ☐
3 Hindley starts drinking and becomes violent and aggressive. ☐ ☐
4 Edgar Linton falls in love with Cathy. ☐ ☐
5 Cathy stops being friends with Heathcliff. ☐ ☐
6 Hareton is killed in an accident. ☐ ☐
7 Cathy refuses to marry Edgar Linton. ☐ ☐
8 Cathy tells Heathcliff she loves him. ☐ ☐
9 Hindley moves away. ☐ ☐
10 Heathcliff leaves Wuthering Heights. ☐ ☐

▶ 4 **8 b** **Now listen and check your answers.**

Chapter Three

'Nelly, I am Heathcliff!'

▶ 4 My story jumps forward to the summer of the next year, Mr Lockwood. On the morning of a fine June day, the last of the Earnshaws was born – my beautiful Hareton. But I am sad to say, Frances did not live long after the birth, and her death sent Hindley mad with despair, and he turned to drink. The servants could not stand his evil, tyrannical behaviour, and soon Joseph and I were the only ones left at the house. I could not bear to leave Hareton, who I took care of as if he were my own. Hindley hardly noticed him.

Hindley's cursing and terrible, violent behaviour was a bad example for Miss Cathy and Heathcliff. The way he treated Heathcliff would have made a devil out of a saint; in fact during this time, Heathcliff almost looked as if he were possessed by a devil. He loved to see Hindley drunk and degraded[1], and every day he, too, became more savage and violent.

The house became a living hell. No one came near us except Edgar Linton, who overcame his terror of Hindley to visit Miss Cathy. At fifteen, she was the queen of the countryside, but she had become so strong-willed[2] and proud that I no longer liked her. She remained fiercely attached to Heathcliff, and Edgar Linton, with all his superiority, found it difficult to enter her heart as deeply as Heathcliff had.

1. **degraded:** 身份降低   2. **strong-willed:** 倔强

Cathy found herself caught between two worlds. When she was with Edgar Linton, she behaved in a more ladylike way, and had to agree with Edgar's criticisms of Heathcliff. Then when Edgar left and Heathcliff was telling her how much he disliked Edgar, she had to agree with him. I do not think she was being deliberately dishonest, but she genuinely did not know how to balance these two sides of her character, or how to behave with her two friends; and she did not like her two friends ever meeting each other.

One day, Hindley was away from the house, and Heathcliff had taken advantage of this to have a holiday from work. He must have been about sixteen at the time. He had sunk[1] very low. He was far from stupid, but although Miss Cathy tried to teach him what she learnt, he could not keep up with her lessons. He had become quite deliberately repulsive[2], as if to keep everyone away from him. He was very different from the man you see today. He stopped showing his affection for Miss Cathy, as if he had already understood the impossibility of his love for her.

On this day, he came into the kitchen as Miss Cathy was getting ready to see Edgar Linton. She was surprised and cross to see Heathcliff, thinking he would be working on the fields.

'I thought we could spend the day together, Cathy,' he said, 'we are not often free of Hindley.' Then he stopped, seeing her in her lovely silk dress, and me making her hair pretty. 'Are you expecting visitors today, then?'

'Isabella and Edgar Linton said they might come, but since it is raining, I do not think they will.'

---

1. sunk: 沉沒的，這裏引申為
無可救藥 ▶FCE◀

2. repulsive: 令人反感

'You spend more time with those Lintons than you do with me!' exclaimed Heathcliff.

'Well, perhaps that is because I find them more interesting than you,' she snapped[1] at him. 'What do you talk about? You might be dumb or a baby for anything you say to interest me, or for anything you do, either!'

'You never told me before that you disliked my company, Cathy!' Heathcliff said, extremely agitated.

'It is no company at all, when people know nothing and say nothing,' she said crossly.

Heathcliff could not answer her, for at that moment we heard a horse's feet on the yard. There was a quiet knock at the door and Edgar came in, his smiling face showing his delight at this unexpected chance to see Cathy without Hindley being at home. Heathcliff left, his face black with rage.

No doubt, at that moment, the contrast between her two friends became more noticeable than ever to Miss Cathy. It was like exchanging a bleak[2], black hillside for a beautiful green valley. Edgar's voice was sweet and gentle, and he did not speak with the rough, harsh accent we have round here.

Hindley had told me I must stay with Miss Cathy if she had a visitor, but she was not happy to see me in the room with her and Edgar, and told me to leave. When I said she would not, she pinched me, and I cried out with the pain.

'Oh Miss, that was a nasty thing to do. You have no right to hurt me like that!' I said.

'I did not touch you, you lying creature,' she said, her eyes filled with passionate rage.

---

1. **snapped:** 突然發怒　　　　　　2. **bleak:** 荒涼

'What's that, then?' I asked, showing her the purple marks on my arm.

At that point, she could not control her anger, and she slapped[1] me on the cheek.

'Catherine, love! Catherine!' said Edgar Linton, shocked.

Little Hareton, who followed me everywhere, and was sitting near me on the floor, started crying when he saw what had happened, and said 'wicked Aunty Cathy'. On hearing this, Cathy took the child and began to shake him violently. Edgar tried to stop her, but then she turned and slapped him. Edgar stood stunned and silent, then he turned to leave.

'That's right,' I thought to myself, 'Let's this be a lesson to you, Edgar Linton. Go now while you still can and never come back.'

'Where are you going?' Cathy said, moving to stand in front of the door. 'You must not go!' she said.

'How can I stay after you have hit me?' he said.

'If you go, you will make me cry, and I shall become so miserable that I shall be ill,' she replied. She dropped down onto her knees and began to sob[2].

Edgar went out into the yard, but then he stopped and looked back towards the house. How I wished he could see how spoilt she was, but he was powerless, and there was no way to save him from his fate. He turned round, went back into the house and shut the door.

When I went in a little while later to tell them that Hindley had come home and was violent and drunk, I saw that the argument had somehow made them closer. They had lost any shyness with each other; indeed, they had changed from being simply friends and had become lovers. Edgar left before Hindley could find him, and Cathy went quickly up to her room.

Hindley came into the house, in a temper, saying the most terrible

1. **slapped:** 掌摑 ▶FCE◀   2. **sob:** 啜泣

things. He threatened to kill me, then he turned his drunken rage on Hareton, because the poor little thing had not run out to greet his father. He picked the child up and said,

'Kiss your father then, Hareton. What! You will not? Kiss me I said or by God I will break your neck.' He started to take the child kicking and screaming up the stairs. Then he heard a noise below him and forgetting he was holding his son, leant over the stair rails[1] to see what the noise had been. At that point Hareton tried to free himself, and he fell out of his father's arms towards the floor below.

Almost before I could understand what was happening, Heathcliff had leapt forward and caught the child in his arms. I took Hareton from Heathcliff, and Hindley came slowly down the stairs.

'This is your fault, Nelly. You should have kept him out of my sight. Is he injured?' he asked quietly.

'Injured?' I cried. 'It is only by a miracle that he is not dead. I am surprised his mother does not rise from her grave[2] to see how you treat her son.'

He tried to touch the child, but I pushed him away.

'You shall not touch him,' I said. 'He hates you – they all hate you – that's the truth! A happy family you have!'

He told us all then to get out of his sight, and when he had gone, Heathcliff said, 'It is a pity he cannot kill himself with drink.'

I went into the kitchen to sing my poor Hareton to sleep, and when Miss Cathy came in to me, I thought Heathcliff had gone out to see to the horses.

'Are you alone, Nelly?' she asked.

'Yes, Miss,' I replied, forgetting her recent behaviour.

She seemed disturbed and anxious.

---

1. **stair rails:** 樓梯扶手   2. **grave:** 墳墓

'Where's Heathcliff?'

'Looking after the horses.'

Heathcliff did not say anything, perhaps he had fallen asleep.

'I want to know what to do, Nelly. Today, Edgar Linton asked me to marry him, and I have given him an answer. Now before I tell you if it was yes or no, you must tell me what you think my answer should have been.'

'Really, Miss Cathy, how can I know that? After your behaviour this afternoon, you should certainly have said no, because if he asked you after that, then he must be hopelessly stupid or a naive fool.'

'If you want to be like that, then I will go away,' she said standing up. Then she changed her mind.

'I said yes, Nelly. Now be quick and tell me if I was wrong.'

'If you said yes, then there is no point in discussing the matter. You have made your promise. Do you love him?'

'Yes.'

'Well, where is the problem?' I asked.

'Here and here!' she answered, striking[1] one hand on her forehead and the other on her heart. 'In my soul and in my heart, I am convinced that I am wrong.' She hesitated a moment. 'Nelly, do you ever dream strange dreams?' I shook my head.

'I do,' she continued. 'I have dreamt in my life, dreams that have stayed with me ever after, and changed my ideas; they've gone through me like wine through water and altered[2] the colour of my mind.'

'Don't tell me,' I said, 'I do not want to hear your dreams.' I have never liked hearing people's dreams, and this time, seeing Miss Cathy look so gloomy, I had a strange feeling, as if the dream she was about to tell me might be a prophecy.

---

1. **striking:** 擊打

2. **altered:** 改變

She stopped, annoyed that I did not want to continue the conversation.

❖ ❖ ❖

Then some minutes later, as if she were changing the subject, she said, 'If I were in heaven, Nelly, I would be extremely miserable.'

'Because you are not fit to go there,' I answered. 'All sinners[1] would be miserable in heaven.'

'It's not for that,' she laughed. 'I dreamt, once, that I was there.'

I got up to leave. I did not want to stay to hear this terrible dream, but she laughed again and made me sit down.

'I was only going to say that heaven did not seem to be my home; and I broke my heart with weeping[2] to come back to the earth. The angels were so angry that they threw me out, right into the middle of the moors above Wuthering Heights where I woke crying with joy. That is where the problem is. I have no more business marrying Edgar Linton than I have to be in heaven, and if that wicked Hindley had not brought Heathcliff so low, I would not have thought of it. Heathcliff is so inferior to me now. I could not marry him.'

At that moment, I saw a shadow move in the doorway and I understood that Heathcliff had heard every word that she said. He left and never heard what she said after that.

'Heathcliff will never know how I love him, and that is not because he is handsome, Nelly, but because he is more myself than I am. Whatever our souls are made of, his and mine are the same. Linton's soul is as different from ours as moonlight from lightning, or ice from fire. But I will never tell him, because he does not understand what love is.'

1. sinners: 罪人   2. weeping: 不停哭

'I see no reason why he should know less about love than you do,' I answered, 'and if you are his choice, then he will be the most unfortunate man alive. Because as soon as you become Mrs Linton, he will lose friend and love and all! Have you considered how you will bear the separation?'

'But Nelly, that will never happen. I will never be separated from Heathcliff. Who will separate us? I will never let Edgar do that. Heathcliff will be as much to me as he has been all my life. Edgar will simply have to learn to like him. I see now, you think I am heartless and selfish, but if I married Heathcliff, we would not have a penny[1]. You have not considered that with my husband's money I can help Heathcliff.'

'With your husband's money?' I said. 'I do not think he will agree to that! That is a terrible reason for marrying Edgar Linton.'

'It is not; it is a wonderful reason. Listen Nelly, my miseries[2] in this world have been Heathcliff's miseries, and I have felt each one from the beginning. My love for Linton is like the leaves on the trees. Time will change it, I know that, as winter changes the trees. But my love for Heathcliff is like the eternal rocks below. Nelly, I am Heathcliff; he is always, always in my mind. So you see, we will never be separated.'

She came in tears to hug me, but I pushed her away. I had lost patience with her foolishness. At that moment, Joseph came in, asking us if we had seen Heathcliff. We went out into the night to call him, but there was no answer.

'I'm afraid, Miss,' I said to Cathy, 'he heard a lot of what you said.'

It was a very dark evening for summer: it looked as though there would be a storm. I said we should go home and that the rain would make Heathcliff come home, but Miss Cathy was extremely worried.

---

1. **penny:** 便士 ▶FCE◀   2. **miseries:** 痛苦

She kept walking to and fro, from the gate to the door, until at last she sat on the wall near the road, where, ignoring the thunder and the rain that had begun to fall, she sat calling and listening, until she started to cry.

About midnight, the storm hit Wuthering Heights with its full fury[1]. There was a violent wind, as well as thunder. Miss Cathy came back in, soaked to the skin. Though I tried to get her to change, she lay down on a chair in her wet clothes and went to sleep.

The next day, she had a fever; the doctor told us she was dangerously ill. I will never forget the scene she made that night. I thought she had gone mad.

'He is gone, Nelly, gone,' she said over and over again.

Cathy became very ill, so Mr and Mrs Linton took her to the Grange, but they both caught her fever and died after only a few days. When Cathy came home, she was more difficult than ever. Heathcliff had not been seen or heard of since the night of the storm, and one day, when I said to her that she was to blame[2] for him going, she stopped speaking to me for several months.

Edgar Linton thought he was the happiest man alive the day that Cathy became his wife, three years after his parents had died.

After they were married, Cathy, now Mrs Linton, asked me to live with them at the Grange, but I did not want to leave Hareton. He was five years old, and I was teaching him to read. But Hindley shouted that he did not want a woman in the house. I had to kiss Hareton goodbye and since that day he has been a stranger[3]. ■

1. **fury:** 暴怒
2. **blame:** 為過失負責 ▶FCE◀

3. **stranger:** 陌生人

Reading Comprehension

1 Who did things happen to? Write the correct codename next to the statements below. Sometimes there is more than one name per sentence.

> Hareton = HA • Cathy = C • Heathcliff = HC • Hindley = HI
> • Frances = F • Edgar = E • Nelly = N

1 He was born. ___

2 She died. ___

3 He became violent and drunk. ___

4 He overcame his terror of him. ___ ___

5 He visited her. ___ ___

6 When she was with him, she behaved in a more ladylike way. ___ ___

7 He became deliberately repulsive. ___

8 He stopped showing his affection to her. ___ ___

9 He saved him. ___ ___

10 He asked her to marry him. ___ ___

11 She told her she could not marry him. ___ ___ ___

12 He left. ___

2 Are the following statements true (T) or false (F)? T F

1 Edgar and Heathcliff became friends. ☐ ☐

2 Edgar was terrified of Hindley. ☐ ☐

3 Hareton was injured in an accident. ☐ ☐

4 Heathcliff wished that Hindley would die. ☐ ☐

5 Cathy told Nelly she was wrong to marry Edgar.

6 Cathy knew that Heathcliff was listening to her conversation with Nelly. ☐ ☐

7 Heathcliff heard everything that Cathy said.

8 Cathy stayed out in the rain calling for Heathcliff ☐ ☐
to come back.

9 Cathy went to Thrushcross Grange, but Isabella ☐ ☐
became ill and died.

10 Cathy married Edgar Linton.

Writing

3 Hareton is nearly killed in a terrible accident. Using the prompts in the box below, write a short summary of the accident.

Hindley	back	Hindley	leans; forgets
Edgar	leaves	Heathcliff	catches
Hindley	violent; picks up; goes up	Nelly	holds; pushes
Hareton	kicks	Hindley	leaves
		Heathcliff	wishes

V

4 Opposites. Fill in the gaps in the second paragraph with words which mean the opposite to the ones in the first paragraph.

Nelly, my **(1)** happy times in this world have been Heathcliff's **(2)** happy times, and I have felt each one from the **(3)** end. My **(4)** hatred for Linton is like the leaves on the trees. Time will change it, I know that, as winter changes the trees. But my love for Heathcliff is like the eternal rocks **(5)** above. Nelly, I am Heathcliff; he is **(6)** never, never in my mind. So you see, we will never **(7)** stay together.

Nelly, my **(1)** _____ in this world have been Heathcliff's **(2)** _____, and I have felt each one from the **(3)** _____. My **(4)** _____ for Linton is like the leaves on the trees. Time will change it, I know that, as winter changes the trees. But my love for Heathcliff is like the eternal rocks **(5)** _____. Nelly, I am Heathcliff; he is **(6)** _____, _____ in my mind. So you see, we will never **(7)** _____.

5 Modal verbs and hypothetical constructions. Fill in the gaps with the correct verb from the box below.

> could • might • must • should • should • would

1 ... you must tell me what you think my answer _____ have been.

2 After your behaviour this afternoon, you _____ certainly have said no.

3 If he asked you after that, then he _____ be hopelessly stupid or a naive fool.

4 I had a strange feeling, as if the dream she was about to tell me _____ be a prophecy.

5 If I were in heaven, Nelly, I _____ be extremely miserable.

6 Heathcliff is so inferior to me now, I _____ not marry him.

6 Choose the best word, A, B, C or D, to complete the following sentences.

1 Edgar came in, his _____ face showing his delight at this unexpected chance to see Cathy.

   A ☐ smile   **C** ☐ smiled

   B ☐ smilingly **D** ☐ smiling

2 The contrast between her two friends became more _____ than ever to Miss Cathy.

   A ☐ noticed   **C** ☐ noticeable

   B ☐ noticing   **D** ☐ notice

3 It was like exchanging a bleak, black hillside for a _____ green valley.

   A ☐ beauty   **C** ☐ beautified

   B ☐ beautician **D** ☐ beautiful

4 'I did not touch you, you _____ creature,' she said.

   A ☐ lying   **C** ☐ liar

   B ☐ lied   **D** ☐ lies

5 I saw that the _____ had somehow made them closer.

   A ☐ argumentative **C** ☐ argue

   B ☐ argument   **D** ☐ argumentation

7a In this chapter is one of the most famous quotations from *Wuthering Heights*. Put the parts of the sentence in the correct order.

and altered the colour of my mind. • dreams that have stayed with me ever after, • they've gone through me like wine through water • I have dreamt in my life, • and changed my ideas;

_____

_____

_____

_____

_____

7b Why do you think this sentence has become so well known?

_____

_____

_____

_____

PRE-READING ACTIVITIES

8a Before you read Chapter Four, write your opinion about the following statements and then discuss your ideas with a partner.

1 Cathy is right to marry Linton.

_____

2 I think they will be happy together.

_____

3 Heathcliff will accept the situation.

_____

4 Cathy and Heathcliff will never see each other again.

_____

5 Heathcliff will marry someone else.

_____

8b Now read and check your answers.

Chapter Four

'Oh, Edgar, Heathcliff has come back!'

 5 For several months Cathy and Edgar seemed happy together, though I saw how careful he and Isabella were not to upset[1] her. There were times when Cathy was silent and depressed, but through all of this her husband remained patient, and when she returned to him like the sunshine, he answered her with his own sunshine. It had to end of course. Our true natures can never be hidden for long.

❖ ❖ ❖

On a warm evening in September, I was coming back from the garden with a basket of apples, when I heard a deep voice.

'Nelly, is that you?'

I saw a tall man near the door.

'Who can it be?' I thought. 'It does not sound like Hindley.'

'I have waited here an hour,' the man said, while I continued staring, 'but I dared not enter. You do not know me? Look, I'm no stranger!'

Out of the shadows stepped a distinguished[2] tall man dressed in dark clothes, with a dark face and hair. I looked more closely at the face, still not recognising the man before me. Then I saw his deep, dark eyes. I remembered the eyes.

---

1. **upset:** 令人難過　　　　　　2. **distinguished:** 氣度不凡的

'What!' I cried. 'Is it really you come back?'

'Are they at home?' he asked. 'I must speak with Cathy. Go and tell her I am here. I am in hell till you do.'

I went back into the house and went into the living room to light the candles. Edgar and Cathy were sitting together, looking out of a window at the garden and the wild green trees beyond. The room, the scene outside, Edgar and Cathy, they all looked so peaceful, that I did not want to tell them who was here.

'A person is here to see you, ma'am[1].'

'Who is it, Nelly?'

'I don't know.'

'Close the curtains and bring our tea while I go and see who it is.'

She left, and Edgar asked innocently who the visitor was.

'Someone my mistress does not expect, sir, that Heathcliff who used to live with Mr Hindley.'

'What? That terrible farm boy? That foreigner?' he exclaimed.

'Oh you must not say that, sir. She would be sad to hear you speak like that: she was heart broken when Heathcliff ran away. She will be so happy that he has come back.'

Edgar went over to a window that overlooked the main entrance and opened it. He looked down to Cathy and Heathcliff and called,

'Don't stand there, love! Bring the person in.'

She came back, bursting into the room in great excitement. She threw her arms round her husband crying, 'Oh, Edgar! Edgar darling, Heathcliff has come back!'

'I don't know why you think him so wonderful,' he said rather crossly.

'Oh, Edgar, I know you did not like him. But for my sake, you must be friends now. Shall I tell him to come in?'

---

1. ma'am: 夫人（僕人對女主人的稱呼）

'Here? Don't you think the kitchen would be a more suitable place?'

'No,' she said. 'I cannot sit in the kitchen. Put two tables here, Nelly, one for your master and Miss Isabella, being gentry[1], and one for Heathcliff and myself, being of a lower class. Or shall we go somewhere else, Edgar?'

She was about to run off again, but Edgar stopped her.

'*You* tell him to come up,' he said, speaking to me. 'And, Catherine, try to be happy without exaggerating. We do not need the whole house to see you welcoming a runaway[2] servant as if he were your brother.'

I went down and found Heathcliff waiting by the door. When we got up to the room, I could see from the red faces of both Edgar and Cathy that they had had an argument[3]. When Heathcliff came in, Cathy stepped forward, held out her hands to her friend and brought him over to greet Edgar.

As he came into the full light of the fire, Edgar was as surprised as I had been at how much Heathcliff had changed. From the violent and dirty farm boy of a few years ago, he had become transformed into a handsome, dignified gentleman, who made Edgar seem quite small.

Edgar did not know how to speak to this man who had once been little more than a servant.

'Sit down, sir,' he said eventually. 'Mrs Linton would like me to greet you warmly, and of course, I am pleased when anything happens to please her.'

'And I also,' answered Heathcliff. 'Especially if what pleases her has anything to do with me.'

He sat down opposite Cathy, who kept her eyes on him as if he would vanish[4]. They were so caught up in each other that they completely forgot about Edgar, who gradually became pale with rage.

---

1. **gentry:**（尤指舊時的）上流社會人士
2. **runaway:** 逃離
3. **argument:** 爭執
4. **vanish:** 突然消失

'I will think this has been a dream tomorrow,' Cathy said passionately. 'I shall not be able to believe that I have seen, and touched and spoken to you once more – and yet, cruel Heathcliff, you do not deserve this welcome. You have been away for three years and have never once thought about me!'

'I have certainly thought of you, more than you have thought of me,' he replied quietly. 'I heard you were married, but I wanted to see you, just for a minute, to see the look of surprise on your face when you saw me, then I would have gone away. But now that you have greeted me so warmly, I shall come again to see you often.'

'Catherine, unless you want to drink cold tea, please come to the table,' interrupted her husband, trying to sound as much like his normal self as possible. Miss Isabella was called to take tea, and I left the room.

The meal was over in less than ten minutes, and as Heathcliff left, I asked him if he were staying in the village.

'No, at Wuthering Heights,' he answered. 'Mr Hindley invited me when I called this morning.'

Hindley had invited him? I could not understand how his old enemy could have invited him, but I had a feeling deep in my heart, that Heathcliff should never have come back.

That night, about midnight Cathy woke me up.

'I cannot rest, Nelly,' she said. 'Edgar is being sulky, but I am so happy. He refuses to speak except to say silly things, saying I am cruel[1] and selfish because I wanted him to talk when he was feeling sick and sleepy. I said a few nice things about Heathcliff, and then he began to cry, so I got up and left him.'

'There is no point in talking to him about Heathcliff,' I said. 'They

1. cruel: 殘忍

never liked each other even when they were boys. Heathcliff would hate it if you praised[1] Edgar to him – it's human nature. I would not talk any more to Mr Linton about it, unless you want to cause a really big argument.'

'But isn't he being weak being so jealous? I am not jealous of Isabella with her blond hair and light skin. Everyone loves her, even you Nelly. If we have an argument, you always say that Isabella was right. I never mind that. No, Edgar and Isabella are like spoilt children: they think the world was made just to please them.'

'You are wrong, Miss Cathy. They are the ones who make sure you are never made unhappy. But I think that if you and your husband have a disagreement about something you both think is important, you will find that he is not weak, but as stubborn[2] as you are.'

'But he is being so childish,' she continued, 'he began to cry when I said that Heathcliff had become a real gentleman, and anyone would be honoured[3] to call him his friend. Well, Edgar will just have to accept Heathcliff, and there is an end to it.'

Heathcliff moved back in to Wuthering Heights and came often to visit Cathy at the Grange. Edgar, seeing his wife so happy, had no choice but to accept the situation. The main problem came from another direction, one that no one could have predicted. Miss Isabella fell in love with the man that Heathcliff had become.

❖ ❖ ❖

One evening, Isabella and Cathy were sitting together. Isabella looked so unhappy that Cathy asked her what was the matter.

'You are so cruel to me,' she said, bursting into tears.

---

1. **praised:** 讚揚
2. **stubborn:** 固執 ▶FCE◀

3. **honoured:** 很榮幸

'What do you mean?' Cathy answered.

'The other day, when we were walking on the moor, you told me to run ahead while you walked with Mr Heathcliff.'

'And that is why you say I am cruel?' said Cathy laughing. 'We did not care whether you stayed with us or not. I simply thought that you would not be interested in anything that Heathcliff had to say.'

'Oh, no,' Isabella wept. 'You deliberately sent me away because you knew how much I wanted to be there.'

'Has she gone mad, Nelly? Listen, Isabella, I will repeat our conversation word for word, and you will see how it could not have interested you at all.'

'It is not the conversation,' she said, 'it is because I want to be with –' she stopped.

'Go on,' said Cathy.

'… because I want to be with *him*, and you send me away because you do not want anyone else to be loved but you.'

'How do you dare[1] be so rude to me!' exclaimed Cathy in surprise. 'But surely this is impossible. Tell me you are not so blind that you think Heathcliff a suitable person to fall in love with, Isabella? If this is true, then you are a fool.'

'I am not,' cried Isabella. 'I love him more than you ever loved Edgar, and he might love me if you would let him.'

'Then I pity[2] you with all my heart.'

And it seemed to me that Cathy spoke with sincerity. 'Nelly, help me to convince her of her madness,' said Cathy. 'Tell her what Heathcliff is; tell her about his rages, his terrible character. Isabella, you only say this because you do not know his true character. Do not believe that under his rough exterior there is hidden a heart of gold,

---

1. dare: 膽敢 ▶FCE◀　　　　　　　　　　　**2. pity:** 同情、憐憫

a gentle soul; no, he is a fierce, pitiless, wolfish man. He would crush you like a bird's egg, Isabella Linton,' she paused and thought for a moment. 'Isabella, be very careful what you do. He has grown to love money, and I am afraid he would be quite capable of marrying you for your money and position.'

We tried to make her change her mind, but she would not listen.

Later that day, Cathy and Isabella were sitting in the drawing room when Heathcliff arrived. I saw a mischievous[1] look on Cathy's face.

'Oh, do come in, Heathcliff, we need someone to come and cheer us up, and you are the person that both of us would choose, isn't that right, Isabella? I am pleased to say that there is someone in this room who adores you even more than I do. My poor sister-in-law is breaking her heart over you.'

Isabella got up to leave, red with embarrassment.

'Oh, you mustn't leave, Isabella,' said Cathy, holding firmly onto her arm. 'She told me that if I moved out of the way, then you would choose to be with her.'

'I think you must be mistaken,' Heathcliff said, sitting down. 'She seems very keen to leave my company now.' And he looked at Isabella as if she were an insect.

The poor girl burst into tears and ran from the room.

'Cathy,' said Heathcliff, as she left the room. 'You weren't speaking the truth, were you?'

'I was. She has been sick with love for you for several weeks. But I will never let you have her, Heathcliff. I like her too much to see her destroyed by you.'

'I have no intention of marrying that girl,' he said.

'She reminds me too much of her brother.' He stopped and

1. **mischievous:** 淘氣頑皮

thought for a moment. 'If you don't have a son, when her brother dies, Isabella will inherit[1] his money and property, won't she?'

'Oh, yes, but Edgar and I will have lots of sons, so they will be the ones who inherit,' Cathy laughed.

❖ ❖ ❖

One day, soon after this, I was in the kitchen when I saw Heathcliff arrive. He found Isabella feeding the doves in the yard behind the house. Heathcliff looked to see if anyone could see them, then he went over to her, laid his hand on her arm and said something to her. She tried to get away, but he held on to her, and looking up again to make sure no one could see, he kissed her.

I was horrified and turned round to see Cathy standing behind me. She had seen what I had.

Unfortunately, Edgar also found out what had happened.

'This situation is unbearable,' he said to me. 'I cannot believe that my wife can call this man her friend. I regret ever letting him into the house.'

That night there was a terrible, violent argument between Edgar and Heathcliff.

'I accepted your visits because it made my wife happy,' Edgar said, 'but your presence here is like a moral poison. You will leave now and never come back.'

'Is this pathetic coward, the man you have chosen over me?' said Heathcliff to Cathy, and he pushed Edgar back in his chair. Edgar stood up then, punched[2] Heathcliff in the throat and left the room.

'You must go now,' said Cathy, 'He will come back with his pistols[3]

---

1. **inherit:** 繼承 ▶FCE◀
2. **punched:** 揮拳猛打 ▶FCE◀

3. **pistols:** 手槍

to shoot you. Go now. He will never let me see you again, and it will be all your fault.'

'I will kill him first. I will crush every bone in his body if I cannot see you,' said Heathcliff.

'You must go, Heathcliff,' I said, looking out of the window, 'Mr Linton is coming back with three servants, and they are armed.'

Heathcliff hesitated, but then, deciding he did not want to have to fight, he left. Cathy called me to follow her upstairs. She was extremely agitated[1].

'Tell my husband that I will not see him. His behaviour towards Heathcliff has made me so upset that I shall stay in my room and not eat. Tell him that I am in danger of becoming seriously ill. If Edgar stops Heathcliff coming here, and I cannot keep Heathcliff for my friend, if Edgar will be mean and jealous, then I will try to break both of their hearts by breaking mine.'

Then she shut herself in her room and refused to come out for several days.

During all this time, Edgar sat stubbornly in his library, reading, and did not ask once about his wife, though he did have a short conversation with Isabella. He tried to convince her of the danger she had placed herself in by loving Heathcliff; he tried to tell her what type of person Heathcliff really was. Isabella Linton did not want to listen or understand what her brother said. She thought he was being authoritarian and small-minded[2]. When she would not promise to forget Heathcliff, Edgar told her that if she ever decided to marry that man, he would have no more contact with her, and she would never see her brother again.

---

1. **agitated:** 焦躁不安   2. **small-minded:** 心胸狭窄

FCE – Reading Comprehension

1 Choose the best answer – A, B, C or D.

1 How do Cathy and Edgar seem after they got married?

A ☐ Content, but they didn't speak to each other much.

B ☐ Happy, but they spent a lot of time with other people.

C ☐ Extremely happy, and everything was perfect.

D ☐ Happy, but Edgar was careful not to upset Cathy.

2 How does Edgar react when Nelly tells him Heathcliff has come back?

A ☐ He accepts him as his wife's friend.

B ☐ He is pleased to see him back.

C ☐ He is shocked.

D ☐ He realises Cathy has never loved him.

3 How does Cathy react to Heathcliff's return?

A ☐ She is extremely excited and ignores Edgar.

B ☐ She is worried that Edgar will not let Heathcliff into the house.

C ☐ She is worried that Heathcliff will upset Edgar.

D ☐ She agrees to see him once, but no more.

4 What does Cathy do when Edgar shows her he is jealous of her relationship with Heathcliff?

A ☐ She tries to reassure her husband that she loves him.

B ☐ She thinks he is being weak and spoilt.

C ☐ She stops loving him.

D ☐ She decides to stop seeing Heathcliff.

5 How does Heathcliff react when Cathy tells him Isabella is in love with him?

A ☐ He doesn't believe her.

B ☐ He is pleased, and he has always loved her.

C ☐ He is surprised and flattered.

D ☐ He says he is too poor to marry her.

6 What does Cathy do when Edgar hits Heathcliff?

A ☐ She gets angry with Isabella for causing the argument.

B ☐ She gets angry with herself for not preventing the argument.

C ☐ She gets angry with Edgar for hitting Heathcliff.

D ☐ She is angry with Heathcliff and does not want to see him again.

Writing

2 The following wordsearch contains 19 words associated with Heathcliff as a young boy and when he returns as a man. As you find them, put each one in the correct part of the table below. Then discover the hidden name.

D	I	G	N	I	F	I	E	D	G	D
N	S	C	O	W	L	I	N	G	E	I
E	R	C	F	A	R	T	R	W	N	S
G	A	H	I	W	A	E	E	O	T	T
L	G	R	E	I	G	I	V	L	L	I
E	E	N	R	C	G	E	E	F	E	N
C	P	P	C	K	E	E	N	I	M	G
T	I	U	E	E	D	A	G	S	A	U
E	T	N	R	D	N	S	E	H	N	I
D	I	I	S	U	L	K	I	N	G	S
T	L	S	H	C	U	R	S	E	D	H
A	E	H	D	E	V	I	L	A	W	E
L	S	E	P	A	T	I	E	N	T	D
L	S	D	H	A	N	D	S	O	M	E

Heathcliff as a boy	Heathcliff when he comes back

3 Using vocabulary from exercise 2, write a letter using the comparative to show how Heathcliff has changed. Write 120-150 words.

4a Put this direct speech into reported speech.

1 'You tell him to come up,' he said, speaking to me.

2 'Sit down, sir,' he said eventually.

3 'I cannot rest, Nelly,' she said to me.

4 'What do you mean?' Cathy answered Isabella.

5 'You must go, Heathcliff,' I said, looking out of the window.

4b Put this reported speech into direct speech.

1 He asked me if they were at home.

2 She asked Nelly who it was.

3 He told her that Mr Hindley had invited him.

4 Isabella said she loved Heathcliff more than Cathy had ever loved Edgar.

Writing

5 Write answers in complete sentences to the following statements, saying if you agree or disagree and giving reasons for your decisions.

1 Edgar is right to be jealous of Heathcliff.

_____

_____

_____

2 Heathcliff has behaved very badly.

_____

_____

_____

3 Cathy's behaviour has been completely innocent.

_____

_____

_____

PRE-READING ACTIVITIES

6a Before you listen, tick the words you think you will hear in the next chapter. Use a dictionary to help you.

stubborn	☐	sorry	☐
silent	☐	tears	☐
shocked	☐	happy	☐
exaggerating	☐	mad	☐
bury	☐	excited	☐
horses' feet	☐	disowned	☐
child	☐	unhappy	☐
fool	☐	torture	☐
divorce	☐	new life	☐
confused	☐	died	☐

▶ 6 **6b** Now listen and check your answers.

Chapter Five

'You and Edgar have broken my heart.'

▶ 6 While Cathy stayed stubbornly locked in her room, and Edgar stayed in his library, buried in his books, Miss Isabella spent most of her time walking around the garden, always silent and almost always in tears[1]. She hardly ate anything and had begun to look quite pale and thin.

Cathy and Edgar, it seemed to me, each waited for the other to be the first to come to them, but both were so stubborn: neither of them would ever be the first to make peace.

I thought there was a little hope in the situation when on the third day Cathy opened her door, saying to me she needed more water and would like to eat something. She ate and drank with appetite, but when she had finished, she lay back on her bed and sighed.

'Oh, I will die,' she exclaimed, 'since no one cares about me. If I die, Edgar will be glad. He does not love me; he would never miss me.'

I admit I was shocked when I saw her. She looked terrible, and she seemed to have become quite mad. But when I saw how eagerly[2] she ate the food I had brought, I honestly did not think that she was in any danger. Indeed, I thought she was deliberately exaggerating her illness in order to make Edgar suffer because he had hit Heathcliff and told him never to come back to the Grange.

1. **in tears:** 哭了起來

2. **eagerly:** 熱切地、渴望地

'I am sure you will not die, ma'am. Do not say such things.'

'And does Mr Linton not worry about me?' she asked. I told her he seemed well and was spending his time in the library with his books because, while she was locked in her room, he did not have anyone else to talk to.

'With his books!' she cried. 'And I dying! Does he not know how changed I am? Nelly, tell him immediately how serious the situation is. Does he really not care if I live or die?'

I repeated that I thought Mr Linton was well.

'If I were sure that it would kill him,' she interrupted me, 'I'd kill myself immediately! The last three nights have been terrible for me. I have not slept at all, and he does not care.'

She continued to say the most awful things, and then she suddenly seemed to go completely mad. She took her pillow[1] and tore it with her teeth so that the feathers flew everywhere. Then she stopped and, talking to herself, she started putting the feathers in a line, according to which bird they had come from. I had never seen her behave so strangely. I remembered what the doctor had said during her last illness, about how no one should upset her, and I began to be worried.

❖ ❖ ❖

A little later, she cried out in fear when she thought she saw a ghost reflected in the mirror, but it was only her own pale, haunted[2] face. Then she began to talk as if she were back in her bed at Wuthering Heights. I believe that she did not know where she was.

It was a cold, moonless night, but she said, 'Open the window, so that I can breathe the clean air from the moors. Look, that's my room with the candle in it.'

---

1. pillow: 枕頭 ▶FCE◀　　　　　　**2. haunted:** 魂不附體似的

As you know, Mr Lockwood, Wuthering Heights cannot be seen from any part of the Grange. 'But I will never go back there,' she continued, 'my last journey will be to the church, and even if they bury me twelve feet under the ground, and put the church on top of me, I will not rest till Heathcliff is with me. I never will!'

Edgar Linton heard our voices, and seeing the door open, came in at last. He was silent. Cathy's appearance[1] had made him too astonished to speak.

'Nelly, why did you not tell me how ill my wife was?' he said, taking her in his arms and looking at her with anguish.

At first, she did not seem to recognise him, then she said angrily, 'Oh you are here, are you, Edgar Linton? You are one of those things that come when they are not wanted, but are never there when you want them!'

'Catherine, what have you done? What has happened? Do you not love me anymore? Do you love that Heath…' but she interrupted him.

'Stop!' she cried, 'If you say that name to me ever again, I will jump from this window.'

There was no logic or reason in what she said. I decided to fetch the doctor, and I left the room with Edgar desperately trying to calm her, speaking to her with endless patience and love.

It was two o'clock in the morning. As I went out of the gate to go to the village, I saw something moving nearby. When I went to look, I saw that Miss Isabella's dog was hanging from a hook[2] with a cloth tied round its neck. It was almost dead. I let it go, and it ran back to the house.

At that moment, I thought I heard the sound of horses' feet galloping away in the night, but I was so worried about Cathy that I did not think anything more about it.

1. appearance: 外貌、樣子　　　　2. hook: 掛鈎

When I came back with the doctor, Edgar had managed to get Cathy to sleep. The doctor examined her, and to our relief, he said he thought that as long as we kept her as calm as possible and did not let her get upset, then she would recover. This was better news than I expected.

I suddenly remembered Miss Isabella's dog. I went to her room but it was empty, and it was then that I understood what had happened. I did not have the courage to tell Edgar.

❖ ❖ ❖

Early the next morning, one of the young servant girls came running into Cathy's bedroom as she slept. 'Master, master, our young lady…' she cried.

'Hush! Speak more quietly, girl,' said Edgar.

The girl, remembering where she was and who she was speaking to, calmed herself and said, 'Our young lady, she's gone, she's gone! Heathcliff's run off with her, and the whole village is talking about it.'

Heathcliff and Isabella had been seen when they had stopped the other side of the village to have a horse's shoe mended[1].

'Shall I send someone after them?' I asked.

'No, Nelly, it was her choice to leave. She had the right to do that,' Edgar said quietly and without emotion. 'Do not speak to me about her again. From now on, she is only my sister in name, not because I disown[2] her, but because she has disowned me.

Oh, Mr Lockwood, if only she had known how ill Cathy was, maybe she would have stayed, and maybe we could have stopped the terrible things that happened next.

❖ ❖ ❖

1. **mended:** 修理   2. **disown:** 與（某人）斷絕關係

Cathy was dangerously ill for two months, and during all that time, Edgar did not leave her side. No mother could have looked after her sick child better than he looked after his wife, and under his patient care, she gradually returned to a fragile health as the winter ended and spring returned. I began to think that she might not die after all. And there was another reason for her to live – she was expecting a child. We hoped that Edgar's heart would soon be made happy by the birth of a son.

Six weeks after she had gone, Isabella sent her brother a note saying she was married to Heathcliff. At the bottom of the note, written in pencil, which I thought was strange, she had added an apology, begging for Edgar's forgiveness[1] and praying for a reconciliation[2]. Edgar did not reply.

Two weeks later, I got a worrying letter from Isabella.

Dear Nelly,

I arrived last night at Wuthering Heights and heard that Catherine has been very ill. Please tell me how she is. I do not want to speak to her directly as I do not wish to upset her. Tell Edgar I would give the world to see his face again.

Oh, Nelly, my life here is terrible. Please visit me as soon as you can. Here is only a horrible old servant man and a filthy child, called Hareton, who swears and curses like an adult. I am told he is my legal nephew, though I can hardly believe it. When I saw him for the first time, he sent his dog to attack me! Then I met Hindley, Cathy's brother. He told me to lock my bedroom door at night, because if he ever found it unlocked, he would come in and shoot Heathcliff dead, and he did not want another death on his conscience.

But the worst thing is this. Heathcliff treats me so badly, Nelly. He

---

1. **forgiveness:** 原諒、寬恕　　　　2. **reconciliation:** 和解

shouts at me and threatens me so much that I have grown to hate him. He has made me so unhappy. I have been a fool! Please come Nelly, but do not tell anyone how bad things are with me. Promise me you won't. I am sure that he treats me like this simply to make Edgar suffer. I would rather die in silence than do anything more to make my brother unhappy. Come soon.'

I did not say a word of what I had read to anyone. The master gave me permission that afternoon to take a few things up to her at Wuthering Heights, and when I arrived, she looked more terrible than I could have imagined, but Heathcliff seemed better than ever! If you did not know them, you would have said she was a farm girl and he a gentleman.

But I will never forget how he spoke that afternoon. He told me in front of her that he despised her, that he had never loved her, and that she was an embarrassment to the name of Linton.

'I am even beginning to get tired of tormenting her. She can leave if she wants,' he ended.

'Do not believe him, Nelly. He is a lying[1] fiend[2], a monster. I tried to leave once, but I do not dare to try again!' she cried.

'Go to your room, woman!' thundered Heathcliff, and he took her by the arm and threw her out.

When she had gone, he said, 'Now, Nelly, you must help me see Cathy again.'

I tried to tell him I would not. I told him how terribly she had changed and how ill she still was, but he went on at me for so long that in the end I agreed to carry a letter to her from him. I did not want to, believe me.

---

1. **lying:** 説謊的   2. **fiend:** 惡魔

I thought that seeing Heathcliff again might kill Cathy this time: her health was still so fragile[1]. I left Wuthering Heights with a heavy heart. I could not bear to think of Isabella in that situation.

That evening, after dark, I saw Heathcliff waiting outside in the garden, but I did not give Cathy the letter then. I waited until the next Sunday, when I was left alone in the house with Cathy while the others went to church. It was a warm day, and she was sitting in a loose, white dress by the open window. Her face had been altered by her illness: when she was calm, she had an unearthly[2] beauty. I gave her the letter, but when she read it, she did not seem to understand it.

'Heathcliff wishes to see you, ma'am.' I explained.

As I said that, I heard his footsteps coming into the house. When he found the room we were in, he went straight over to her and held her tightly for many minutes, kissing her more times than he had ever kissed her in his life, but he could not bear to look at her. He had seen in her face, as I had, that there was no hope of recovery for her.

'Oh, Cathy! Oh, my life! How can I bear it?' he said.

Cathy turned to him and said, 'You and Edgar have broken my heart, Heathcliff, but you both say you are the ones to be pitied. I shall not pity you! You will live long after I am gone. I wish I could hold you till we were both dead! I wouldn't care what you suffered! You will forget me when I am gone. You will come to my grave and say, "That is the grave of Catherine Linton. I loved her once, but I have a new life now."'

'Stop!' he said. 'Do not torture me until I am as mad as you are! Are you possessed by a devil that you can even think to speak to me

1. fragile: 脆弱　　　　　　　　　　　　2. unearthly: 脱俗

like that? You lie when you say that I have killed you. You know you do, and you know that I could forget myself more easily than I could ever forget you.'

Heathcliff stood up and went over to the fireplace, his back to us so that we would not see the great emotion on his face.

'Come here, Heathcliff, come back to me,' and as she said this, she tried to stand up, but she was so weak that she could not. In a flash, Heathcliff caught her, and carried her over to a chair, where he held her in his arms. Time was passing, and I was worried that Edgar would be coming back from church. I told Heathcliff it was time for him to go.

'I must go, Cathy,' said Heathcliff, trying to release himself from her arms, 'but I will come again before you are asleep, and I will stay by your window all night.' Cathy looked at him with mad determination on her face,

'No!' she shrieked[1]. 'Oh, don't, don't go. It is the last time! Edgar will not hurt us!'

'Hush[2], my darling! Hush, hush, Catherine! I'll stay,' said Heathcliff, sinking back down into the chair.

'Are you going to listen to her madness?' I cried. 'Get up and go now. Don't listen to her.' But Cathy had fallen back into Heathcliff's arms, apparently lifeless.

That was how Edgar found them when he came in. When he saw who was in the room with his wife, his face went white with astonishment and rage, but Heathcliff had picked Cathy up, and he took her over to Edgar and placed her in her husband's arms.

'Unless you are a fiend, help her first,' he said. 'Then you will speak to me,' and he left the room.

---

1. **shrieked:** 尖叫

2. **hush:** （示意某人安静）嘘

Edgar and I did everything we could for her, to make her as comfortable and calm as we could. Eventually she did open her eyes again, but she was confused[1], could not speak, and did not recognise anyone.

Edgar seemed to have forgotten about Heathcliff, but I had not. As soon as I had an opportunity to leave the room, I went to find him. He was sitting in a room downstairs. I told him that she was better and that he must now leave.

'I will leave the house,' he answered, 'but I will stay in the garden, and I will come and see her again tomorrow. You must promise to tell me when she is on her own. If you don't, then I will come anyway, whether Edgar is there or not.' And he went out into the dark beyond the house.

That night, about midnight, the Catherine you saw at Wuthering Heights was born, and two hours later, her mother died, never having recovered enough consciousness[2] to miss Heathcliff or to recognise Edgar.

---

1. confused: 困惑

2. consciousness: 意識

Reading Comprehension

1 **Put these events from Chapter 5 in the correct order.**

A ☐ Nelly goes to get the doctor and hears horses' feet galloping away in the night.

B ☐ Nelly visits Wuthering Heights and sees how badly Heathcliff treats Isabella.

C ☐ Cathy stays in her room and Edgar in the library.

D ☐ Nelly and Edgar are shocked by how ill Cathy is.

E ☐ Heathcliff visits Cathy and understands that she is dying.

F ☐ Cathy is expecting a child.

G ☐ They discover that Isabella has run away with Heathcliff.

H ☐ The baby is born and Cathy dies.

I ☐ Edgar finds Heathcliff with Cathy.

J ☐ Isabella walks around the garden, crying.

K ☐ Nelly gets a letter from Isabella who tells her how unhappy she is.

Grammar

2 **Correct the following statements using evidence from the text and the emphatic do/does where appropriate.**

1 Isabella knows how ill Cathy is when she leaves with Heathcliff.
_____

2 Edgar refuses to look after Cathy and is impatient with her.
_____

3 Isabella does not care that she has upset her brother.
_____

4 Isabella finds life at Wuthering Heights difficult at first, but is beginning to enjoy it.
_____

5 Isabella is free to leave Wuthering Heights whenever she likes.
_____

6 Cathy recognises Edgar before she dies.
_____

Vocabulary

3 Fill in the gaps in the following two paragraphs taken from Chapter 5, using words from the box below. The first paragraph has a more positive tone, while the other is more negative.

> terrible • horrible • managed • relief • upset • recover • swears • better • ill • filthy • calm • curses

When I came back with the doctor, Edgar had **(1)** _____ to get Cathy to sleep. The doctor examined her, and to our **(2)** _____, he said he thought that as long as we kept her as **(3)** _____ as possible and did not let her get upset, then she would **(4)** _____. This was **(5)** _____ news than I expected.

Dear Nelly,
I arrived last night at Wuthering Heights and heard that Catherine has been very **(1)** _____. *Please tell me how she is. I do not want to speak to her directly as I do not wish to* **(2)** _____ *her. Tell Edgar I would give the world to see his face again. Oh, Nelly, my life here is* **(3)** _____. *Please visit me as soon as you can. Here is only a* **(4)** _____ *old servant man and a* **(5)** _____ *child, called Hareton, who* **(6)** _____ *and* **(7)** _____ *like an adult.*

Speaking

4 How do you feel when you read these paragraphs? Is the language effective at conveying meaning? Discuss your answers in pairs.

FCE - Writing

5 Isabella receives a letter from a friend who is worried about her. Write Isabella's reply to her friend, saying what has happened to her since she fell in love with Heathcliff. Write 120-180 words.

Grammar

6 a Change the following questions into statements, and the statements into questions.

1 'Does Mr Linton not worry about me?'

_____

2 'Nelly, tell him immediately how serious the situation is.'

_____

3 'Do you not love me any more?'

_____

4 Shall I send someone after them?'

_____

5 'Go to your room, woman!'

_____

6 'I will come and see her again tomorrow.'

_____

6 b Now decide how the meaning has changed. For example, is the sentence or question you have written more or less dramatic, more or less polite?

1 _____ **4** _____

2 _____ **5** _____

3 _____ **6** _____

7 Simple past and past perfect. Choose the correct verb and tense, and fill in the gaps in the sentences below.

1 I_____ her some food, and when I_____ back, I saw she _____ it all. *(give, come, eat)*

2 I _____ what the doctor _____ during her last illness. *(remember, say)*

3 When I _____ back with the doctor, Edgar _____ to get Cathy to sleep. *(come, manage)*

4 When I could not find Isabella, I _____ what _____. *(understand, happen)*

5 He _____ that there _____ no hope of recovery for her. *(see, be)*

76

Speaking

8 **Which of the following characters do you have sympathy for? Why? Why not? Using evidence from the text, write notes, and then discuss your ideas in pairs.**

- Cathy
- Isabella
- Edgar
- Heathcliff

PRE-READING ACTIVITIES

Writing

9a **Using some of the words in the box below, write what you think will happen to each of the characters in the next chapter.**

anger • baby son • cousin • curious • crying • exhaustion • despair • die • grow up • Hareton • Hindley • inquisitive • move to the south • run away • say goodbye • Wuthering Heights

Baby Catherine
_____
_____

Edgar
_____
_____

Heathcliff
_____
_____

Isabella
_____
_____

9b **Now read and check your answers. Did anything surprise you?**

Chapter Six

'She does not need your tears!'

▶ 7 The baby Catherine was a weak child, born after only seven months. It cried constantly, but we were so taken over with the grief[1] of her mother's death that we hardly heard it. We made up for the neglect[2] afterwards, but its beginning was as friendless as its end is likely to be.

When I look back over all those years, I can still hardly bear to think about Edgar's despair at losing his beloved wife; his eyes were sunken with grief. That first night after she died, he laid his head on the pillow next to her. I will never forget the contrast between Edgar and Cathy on the dawn of that first morning. His young, pale face was almost as death-like as hers, and his eyes did not move any more than hers. His was the face of a man exhausted with anguish, but hers showed perfect peace. Her forehead was smooth, her eyes closed, and there was a smile on her lips. No angel in heaven could be more beautiful than she was in that moment. She was free of her suffering, and that made me glad.

As the morning came, I saw that Edgar slept, so I left the house to find Heathcliff, who I knew would be waiting in the garden. I wanted to tell him Cathy had died, but I was afraid to. I did not know what effect the news would have on him.

1. **grief:** （尤指某人之死引起的）傷痛　　2. **neglect:** 疏忽

I found Heathcliff leaning against a great ash tree, and as I approached, he said, 'She is dead. I did not need you to tell me that. Put your handkerchief away, and stop crying. I will not hear your noise. Damn¹ you all! She does not need *your* tears!'

I was weeping as much for him as for her. I pitied him, though there never had been any pity in his heart, either for himself or for others. He remained silent, though on his face I saw his inner agony, while his eyes looked at me with a ferocious stare.

'How did she die?' he asked at last.

'Quietly as a lamb,' I answered. 'She lies now with a sweet smile on her face, as if entering heaven in a gentle dream.'

'May she wake in torment!' he exclaimed. 'You cared nothing for my sufferings, you said. Well, I hope that you will not rest until I also die! You said I murdered you, haunt me then! The murdered *do* haunt their murderers. I know that ghosts walk this earth! Don't leave me. Drive me mad², but do not leave me in this abyss where I cannot find you. I cannot live without my soul.'

As he said this, he hit his head against the tree until blood poured from him. I was appalled. When he saw me watching, he thundered at me to go.

Mrs Linton was to be buried on the Friday, till then she lay in an open coffin. Edgar spent his days and nights there, until one night, exhaustion forced him to go and rest. I had not seen Heathcliff, though I knew he was waiting to say goodbye to her. As I went up to bed, I left a window open in the room that the coffin was in. In the morning, the only sign he had been there was a lock of golden hair on the floor, which had been taken from the locket³ around her neck. I opened it, and found it had been replaced with a lock of Heathcliff's

---

1. **Damn:** （俚語）該死、可惡
2. **drive me mad:** 使（我）發瘋、惱怒

3. **locket:** 盒式吊墜（內有圖片或頭髮，常墜在項鏈上）

own dark hair. I reclosed it and re-arranged Cathy's hair, so that no one could see that he had been.

Hindley was invited to the funeral, but he did not come and did not send any message. Isabella was not invited.

The day after the funeral, the early spring weather had turned back into winter. Edgar was in his room, and I was sitting in a downstairs room with the baby, rocking it gently as it moaned on my lap, when someone came running into the room, laughing. I was shocked. This house was no place for laughter. I was even more shocked when I saw it was Isabella. She stood shivering in soaking wet clothes.

'I mean no disrespect to dear Catherine. I will miss her as much as anyone, but I am glad that *he* suffers,' she said, and with that she took off her wedding ring and smashed it with the poker[1] from the fire. 'I have run the whole way from Wuthering Heights to escape him. I would love nothing more than to stay here with you all and help with the baby, but Heathcliff would never let me be happy in that way. Get the coachman to prepare the coach, Nelly, and get me some dry clothes, I will leave immediately and go somewhere to the south, where I hope he will not be able to find me.'

She left later that afternoon, and I did not see her again. Edgar and she did write to each other, and we learnt that a few months after her escape, she had a son who she called Linton.

Six months after Catherine died, we learnt of Hindley's death. He was only twenty-seven, but he had succeeded in killing himself with his drinking, as Heathcliff had wished all those years before. Not only

---

1. **poker:** 撥火棍 ▶FCE◀

that, but everything he had owned now belonged to Heathcliff, who had lent him money to pay for his drink and his gambling[1]. I was hit hard by Hindley's death: we had grown up together. I wept for him as if he were my own brother.

❖ ❖ ❖

The twelve years that followed were the happiest of my life. I spent my time looking after little Catherine, and she was the loveliest thing, bringing sunshine into a desolate house. She was a real beauty, with the Earnshaws' handsome, dark eyes, but the fair skin and curly blond hair of the Lintons. She was lively, spirited and loving, as her mother had been, but did not inherit her mother's wildness. She had a gentle voice and a thoughtful expression, her anger was never furious, and her love was not fierce, but deep and tender. In all of those things, she was like her father. She had her faults though, she could be very spoilt, but her father was never cross with her.

She never left the house or the great park[2] that surrounded it, apart from once or twice, when Mr Linton took her a short distance outside, but he would not trust her to go that far with anyone else. Wuthering Heights and Heathcliff did not exist for her, as they were never mentioned. She seemed perfectly happy, though sometimes she would look out of her window up to the hills and moors beyond the Grange, and she would say,

'Nelly, how long will it be before I can walk to the top of those hills? What is behind them? Is it the sea?'

'No, Miss Catherine, there are more hills, just like these,' I answered.

---

1. **gambling:** 賭博

2. **park:** 莊園

'And what are those golden rocks like when you stand under them?'

The steep cliff of rocks that was called Penistone Crags[1], a mile or so beyond Wuthering Heights, particularly attracted her, especially when the setting sun shone on it, and the rest of the land lay in shadow.

'Why are they so bright when we are in shadow?' she asked.

'Because they are much higher up than us. You cannot climb them though, they are much too steep for that.'

'Oh, so you have been there, Nelly! Then I can go when I am a woman.'

'They are nothing special,' I said, 'It is much nicer here, Miss,' not wanting to encourage her curiosity.

But one of the servant girls told her about the Fairy[2] cave that was at the bottom of the crag, and from then on Catherine was always talking about going there. Every time she asked her father if she was old enough to go there yet, all he said was, 'Not yet, love, not yet.' The road to the Crags ran past Wuthering Heights, and Edgar did not want her going anywhere near there.

Thirteen years after Catherine died, Isabella wrote to Edgar saying she was very ill. He went to her immediately and was away for three weeks. For the first few days, Catherine missed her father terribly and followed me around the house. I suggested she should ride her pony in the Park and come back to tell me her adventures. She agreed. One day she said she was going on a long journey and would need food and drink. I thought she was playing a game. I did not imagine that she was planning to go up onto the moors.

1. **Crags:** 懸崖、峭壁   2. **Fairy:** 仙子

When Catherine did not come back for tea, I got concerned. I sent servants to look for her in the Park, but we did not find her. I suddenly thought she might have taken advantage of her father's absence and gone to Penistone Crags. I started out immediately to walk the four miles to Wuthering Heights.

And that is where I found her. Her hat was hung on the wall, and she was sitting in a rocking chair[1] that had been her mother's. She looked perfectly at home. She was laughing and chattering to Hareton. Hareton, now a great, strong lad of eighteen, though he was dressed as usual like a farm worker, his clothes and face dirty and his hair unbrushed, stared at her with astonishment and curiosity.

'Ah, Nelly, so you have found me,' she said. 'Have you ever been here in your life?'

'Put your hat on and come home at once,' I cried out trying to take hold of her, but she ran away from me. Hareton and the housekeeper they had there at that time began to laugh, and when Miss Catherine began to laugh too, I said angrily, 'Well, you wouldn't be so pleased to stay here if you knew whose house this was!'

'It's your father's, isn't it?' she said to Hareton.

'No,' he said, blushing[2] with embarrassment.

'Well, are you a servant here, then?'

Hareton grew as black as a thunder cloud when he heard her say that. After several more minutes, I managed to persuade her to leave, and she said to Hareton, as if she were speaking to a servant,

'Now, get my horse. What's the matter? Get my horse I say.'

'I'll see you damned before I am ever *your* servant,' he said, to Miss Catherine's astonishment. No one had ever spoken to her like that before.

---

1. **rocking chair:** 搖椅   2. **blushing:** 臉紅

'Hush now, Miss Catherine, you should not be speaking to your cousin like that,' I said.

'My cousin? He's not my cousin. My father has gone to get him from London,' she said, '*he* is a gentleman's son,' horrified that this filthy[1] young man could be her cousin, and she began to cry. Hareton in the meantime, feeling sorry for her, went to get her horse. When she took the horse from him, she looked at him again in horror.

I had to smile at her behaviour. Hareton was tall and well built, handsome in face, but he was dressed in clothes suited for working on the farm or catching rabbits up on the moors. I was pleased to see that my little Hareton had not been so badly mistreated by Heathcliff, though he had not been given any advantages either. You could see that he had better qualities than his father, Hindley, though I discovered that he had never been taught to read or write, and if he ever used bad language, no one told him it was wrong.

Hareton went to get a little puppy to give to Catherine, but she refused his gift, and we went back home, both of us silent and unhappy.

Later, when I tried to get her to tell me what she had been doing all day, she was still cross with me and would only tell me a few details.

She had been going to Penistone Crags. As she passed Wuthering Heights, Hareton had been coming out of the gate with his dogs, who had frightened her horse with their barking[2]. Hareton managed to calm the dogs, and Catherine explained who she was and where she was going, and asked him to show her the way.

He had shown her the Fairy cave at the bottom of Penistone Crags and twenty other secret places, but she did not tell me more about the day she had spent with Hareton. I understood that she had liked him well enough before she had found out he was her cousin!

1. **filthy:** 骯髒   2. **barking:** 狗吠聲

I told her then not to say anything to her father about what had happened. I said how much he disliked everyone at Wuthering Heights and how sorry he would be to find she had been there. Then, when I told her I thought her father would send me away if he found out I had not been looking after her properly, she promised not to say a word. She could not bear it if I was not there any more. She was really a sweet little girl.

❖ ❖ ❖

A letter, announcing Isabella's death, told us the date of Edgar's return and the arrival of Catherine's cousin, Linton, who would be living with us at the Grange. Catherine was wild with excitement about her father's return and about meeting her cousin.

'Linton is only six months younger than I am,' she chattered to me, 'It will be so lovely to have him as my new friend. Aunt Isabella once sent Papa a lock of his hair; it was even more blond than mine. I kept it in a little box and often thought how nice it would be to meet the person the hair belonged to.'

We went to wait for them at the gate, with Catherine running backwards and forwards ahead of me.

Catherine shrieked when she saw her father's face in the carriage[1], and he was as excited to see her. While they chatted and hugged and kissed each other, I looked into the other window of the carriage to see Linton.

He was asleep in a corner, wrapped in a warm, fur-lined cloak as if it were winter. He looked a pale, thin boy, more like Edgar's younger brother. I admit I did not much like him when I saw him, but

---

1. carriage:（尤指舊時的）四輪馬車

I still hoped his father did not find out that he was here. I was afraid Heathcliff would take him from us to live at Wuthering Heights.

Catherine and her father walked back, while Linton continued to sleep in the carriage to the Grange. When they arrived at the house, Edgar said to his daughter,

'Now, darling, your cousin is not as strong or high-spirited as you are, and he has lost his mother very recently, so you must be gentle and leave him in peace. Don't tire[1] him by talking too much this evening.'

When the carriage arrived, Edgar lifted the boy out to meet Catherine.

'This is your cousin Catherine, Linton. She likes you already, so try to stay cheerful and do not cry tonight. The journey is over now; all you have to do is rest.'

'Then let me go to bed,' said the boy, beginning to cry immediately.

Edgar carried him into the drawing room[2], and told him to sit on a chair.

'I can't sit on a chair,' he said, tears running down his face. We put him on a sofa, and I took him his tea there. Catherine brought a little stool and sat beside him quietly. She soon began to stroke his hair and brush away his tears. He seemed pleased by this and gave a weak smile.

Later, when everyone had gone to bed, Joseph came walking straight into the house.

'I must speak with Master Edgar,' he said, 'I have come to take Linton to Wuthering Heights, and I will not leave till I have him.'

1. **tire:** 令人疲倦

2. **drawing room:** 客廳、起居室

Reading Comprehension

1 **Who, where or what? Answer the following questions about Chapter 6. You do not need to write complete sentences.**

1 Who lay next to Cathy after she died?

_____

2 Where was Cathy's body put before her funeral?

_____

3 What was Cathy wearing round her neck?

_____

4 Who came to say goodbye to Cathy?

_____

5 What did Nelly find on the floor the next morning?

_____

6 Who came running into Thrushcross Grange the day after the funeral?

_____

7 Who died soon after Cathy?

_____

8 Who had a baby boy?

_____

9 What was his name?

_____

10 Where did young Catherine go when she was twelve?

_____

11 Who did she meet?

_____

12 What was his relationship to her?

_____

13 Who came to stay at Thrushcross Grange when his mother died?

_____

14 Who came to take him away?

_____

FCE – Grammar

2 Fill in the gaps in the following paragraph using one word.

'Now, darling, **(1)** _____ cousin is not **(2)** _____ strong or high-spirited **(3)** _____ you are, and he has lost **(4)** _____ mother very recently, so you must be gentle and leave him **(5)** _____ peace. Don't tire him **(6)** _____ talking too much this evening.'
When the carriage arrived, Edgar lifted the boy **(7)** _____ to meet Catherine.
'This is your cousin Catherine, Linton. She likes you already, **(8)** _____ try to stay cheerful and **(9)** _____ not cry tonight. The journey is **(10)** _____ now; all you have to do is rest.'

3a Fill in the gaps in this paragraph using the gerund and verbs as nouns, and report information by using the correct tense.

announce • arrive • be • live • meet • return • return • tell

A letter, **(1)**_____ Isabella's death, **(2)**_____ us the date of Edgar's **(3)**_____ and the **(4)**_____ of Catherine's cousin, Linton, who **(5)**_____ with us at the Grange. Catherine **(6)**_____ wild with excitement about her father's **(7)**_____ and about **(8)**_____ her cousin.

3b Now give the name of the structure or tense for each of the verbs. Choose from the options below.

future • reported future continuous •
gerund • noun • simple past

1 _____
2 _____
3 _____
4 _____
5 _____
6 _____
7 _____
8 _____

Vocabulary

4 Solve these anagrams used to describe the young Catherine as a girl.

1 SOETLVELI   _____
2 TAEUYB   _____
3 YVLLIE   _____
4 SIITPRED   _____
5 TLENGE   _____
6 HTGTFHOUUL   _____
7 EETNDR   _____
8 PSLTOI   _____

5 Fill in the crossword below to find out what Catherine and Hareton did when they spent the day together.

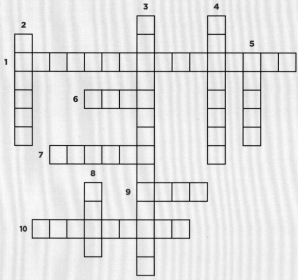

1 Hareton's house.
2 ... secret places.
3 Name of steep rocks.
4 The dogs ... the horse.
5 Catherine's animal.
6 Hareton's animals.
7 Hareton is Catherine's ...
8 Dog noise.
9 Hareton managed to ... the dogs.
10 At the bottom of the rocks.

Speaking

6 **Speaking practice. Choose someone you like. It could be a friend or a member of your family. Work in pairs, describing to each other the person you have chosen and using some of the words from this exercise.**

7 **Think about the following questions, then discuss your answers in pairs.**

- Is Isabella right to run away?
- Do you think women within marriage have more rights today?
- Do you like the young Catherine? Why? Why not?
- Do you like Linton? Why? Why not?
- What do you think of Hareton?

PRE-READING ACTIVITIES

8a **Before you listen, tick all the sentences you think you will hear in the next chapter.**

1 You must not tell Catherine where he has gone. ☐

2 I cannot let them see each other. ☐

3 I will be happy for Catherine to meet Heathcliff. ☐

4 Why did Mamma never speak about my father? ☐

5 Heathcliff was happy to see his son for the first time. ☐

6 Linton hid his face in my shoulder and began to cry. ☐

7 Heathcliff was proud of his son. ☐

8 I want her to see Linton, and I am sure we can make her keep the visit a secret. ☐

9 Catherine was pleased that Hareton was her cousin, but she wished she had never met Linton. ☐

▶ 8 **8b** **Now listen and check your answers.**

Chapter Seven

'Don't leave me! I'll not stay here!'

▶ 8 We knew that Heathcliff would not rest until he had got his son back, and when I told Edgar about Joseph, he told me to take the boy to Wuthering Heights the next morning before the rest of the house was awake.

'I do not wish him to go to his father's house. It was not what I had hoped for him,' Edgar said, 'but we have no choice. Since we will have no influence[1] over his destiny[2], good or bad, you must not tell Catherine where he has gone, and I cannot let them see each other or be friends. If she does not know where he is, then she will not be tempted to go to Wuthering Heights. I will not have her come into contact with that terrible man. Tell her only, that Linton's father has asked to see him, and he has had to leave immediately.'

Linton was not pleased when I woke him the next morning at five o'clock, and he was astonished when I told him to get ready for another journey. I told him his father was anxious to see him as soon as possible.

'My father?' he asked, confused. 'Mamma never told me I had a father. Where does he live? I'd rather stay with Uncle Edgar.'

I am sorry to say I lied to Linton.

1. **influence:** 影響   2. **destiny:** 命運

'He does not live far away, just over those hills, so you will be able to come and visit us often,' I said, though I knew this would never happen. 'You must try to love your father, as you loved your mother, then he will love you.'

'But why have I not heard of him before?' the boy continued, 'And why didn't Mamma and my father live together as other people do?'

I told him his mother's health meant she had to move to the south where it was warmer, and that his father had been too busy with work to be able to make the long journey to London.

'Why did Mamma never speak to me about him? She often spoke about Uncle Edgar, and I learnt to love him a long time ago. How will I love my father? I don't know him.'

Linton lay back on his bed, refusing to leave his uncle and cousin, but by telling him I was sure he would not be away for long, and making other false promises, I managed to persuade him to make the journey.

The fresh air, scented with heather[1], the bright sunshine and his enjoyment of riding Catherine's pony had a positive effect on Linton, and he began to feel much better.

'Is Wuthering Heights as lovely as Thrushcross Grange?' he asked, looking back towards the great house sitting peacefully in its green valley.

'There are not as many trees,' I answered, 'and it is not as large, but you have beautiful views of the country from up there, and the air will be better for your health, fresher and drier. You will be able to explore the moors and find all its secret treasures,' I continued. 'Hareton Earnshaw, your other cousin, will be able to show you those.'

'Is my father as young and handsome[2] as Uncle?' he asked.

'He is as young,' I replied, 'but his hair and eyes are dark, and he is

---

1. **heather:** 石南屬的植物   2. **handsome:** 英俊

much taller and bigger than Mr Linton. He will not seem so gentle and kind to you at first, but I am sure with time he will come to love you.'

'Black hair and black eyes? Then I am not much like him,' he said, thoughtfully.

'Not much,' I said. Not at all, I thought, looking at the thin, pale, lifeless boy who rode beside me.

❖ ❖ ❖

When we arrived at the house, it was half past six. I opened the door to the kitchen and found the family had just finished breakfast.

'Hello, Nelly,' cried Mr Heathcliff. 'I thought I might have to come to the Grange myself to claim my property[1], but I am glad to see you have saved me the trouble. Let me have a look at him then.'

He got up and strode[2] over to the door, Hareton and Joseph following. Poor Linton looked at the three of them, quite frightened, while they simply stared at him.

'It looks as if Mr Linton has sent his daughter instead of your son,' Joseph said, shaking his head.

Heathcliff laughed unkindly.

'God! What a beauty! What have they been feeding him, Nelly? This is worse than I expected.'

I helped the trembling child from his horse. With the growing realisation that the man who spoke was his father, Linton hid his face in my shoulder and began to cry.

Heathcliff pulled the boy towards him, then holding his head up by the chin, said, 'You are your mother's son, that is for sure, but I cannot see any of me in you. Now, stop your crying, we will not hurt you. You have heard of me, haven't you?'

---

1. **property:** 財產 ▶FCE◀   2. **strode:** 大步、闊步

'No!' said Linton, his eyes full of fear.

'No? Your mother was wrong not to tell you about me. Well, I am your father, and your mother was a wicked, disrespectful woman not to tell you what kind of father you had. Now, Nelly,' he said, turning to me. 'Sit down and rest before you go back.'

'I hope you will be kind to the boy, Mr Heathcliff,' I said, 'He is the only family you have in the world.'

'I'll be *very* kind to him,' said Heathcliff, laughing. 'Joseph, bring the boy some breakfast. Hareton, what are you standing here for? Get to your work!'

When they were gone, he continued to me.

'Now that his mother and uncle are dead, my son will inherit Thrushcross Grange. I do not want him to die before I see him become its owner, so I will make sure he stays alive because I want the triumph of seeing *my* son become lord of all these estates[1], above the Lintons. I cannot stand the boy, and I hate him because he reminds me of his mother, but I will look after him. I have asked a tutor[2] to come to the house three times a week, and I have told Hareton to obey him. I am sorry though,' he said, looking through the door into the house, 'that the boy is such a disappointment.'

As he was speaking, Joseph placed a bowl of porridge in front of Linton. The child looked at it in horror and pushed the bowl away, saying crossly,

'I will not eat it. Take it away!'

I suggested they should prepare boiled milk or tea for the boy. To my surprise, Heathcliff did not get angry, but sent the housekeeper to the kitchen to get it ready. I thought perhaps Heathcliff had decided to be kind to the boy after all.

---

1. estates: 房地產、莊園   **2. tutor:** 私人導師

Linton was stroking a friendly sheepdog which had come to see him, so while he wasn't looking, I left. But as I closed the door, I heard a cry and the frantic[1] words, 'Don't leave me! I'll not stay here! I'll not stay here!' But they did not let him come out. I got onto Catherine's pony and left as quickly as I could.

When Miss Catherine found that her cousin had gone before she could even get to know him, she was terribly upset. Her father promised her she would see him again, but I knew that was never going to happen. When I went into the village, I sometimes saw the housekeeper from Wuthering Heights. She said Linton's health was weak, and that he complained and whined[2]. Heathcliff seemed to like him less and less, though he tried not to show it to the boy, and did not spend more than a few minutes in the same room as him. Linton was never shown any sympathy, and as a result, he had become selfish and disagreeable. I wished he could have lived with us.

Time passed, and to tell the truth, we mostly forgot about Linton. It was the twentieth of March, Catherine's sixteenth birthday, but because that day was also the anniversary of her mother's death, we never celebrated it. Each year on this day, Edgar would spend the whole day in the library and then, towards evening, he would walk to the church to visit his wife's grave, where he would often stay until after midnight. Catherine had to find something to do.

It was a beautiful day. Catherine came down in the morning dressed for going out. She said her father had allowed her to go to the edge of the moors with me.

I did not question what she said, and we were soon on our walk,

---

1. frantic: 發狂、情緒失控　　　　**2. whined:** （尤指小孩）不停嘀咕

with Catherine bounding ahead of me like a young puppy. The birds were singing, the sun shining, and I was pleased to see Catherine so happy, her golden ringlets flying behind her as she ran, her cheeks as soft and pink as a wild rose, and her eyes as radiant as a clear-blue sky. She was a happy creature in those days. I just wish she had not been such a curious, inquisitive[1] child.

She began to run further and further ahead of me, and I became tired with all the walking. I shouted at her to stop, but she was so far ahead that she could not hear me. She soon disappeared down the far side of a hill, and I hurried to try to catch her. These moors belonged to Mr Heathcliff, and I did not want her to meet him by accident. Eventually, I climbed to the top of the hill, and looking down I saw that Catherine had been stopped by two people. I was sure, by his height, that one of them was Heathcliff, and the other must be Hareton. I began to run.

When I got to them, Heathcliff looked at me with a cruel smile. He had worked out who she was.

'Who are you?' asked Catherine, looking up this man she had never seen before. 'And this man,' she said, looking up at Hareton, 'I have seen him before. Is he your son?'

'No, he is not,' answered Heathcliff. 'But I do have a son, and you have met him before too. Why don't you both come and rest in my house before going back home?'

I whispered to Catherine that we must go straight home. If we went to Wuthering Heights, we would be back late, and her father would be worried.

'Oh, Nelly, I am tired of running,' she answered. 'Let's go and rest. I do not think I have met this man's son, but I am sure the house he is talking about is that one I visited when I came back from Penistone Crags.'

---

1. **inquisitive:** 好問的、愛鑽研的

'It is,' said Heathcliff. 'Now be quiet, Nelly, and let's go. Hareton, you go ahead with Miss Catherine.'

'Mr Heathcliff, this is wrong. She will see Linton again, and she will tell her father.'

'I want her to see Linton, and I am sure we can make her keep the visit a secret. Nelly, I will tell you my plan. I want Linton and Catherine to fall in love. When her father dies, Catherine will no longer have a home: Thrushcross Grange will belong to Linton; that way her future will be more secure.'

I was horrified. I was sure that Catherine's future happiness was not part of Heathcliff's plans. I was convinced that he was motivated by revenge[1] against her father.

When we arrived at the house, Linton was standing in front of the fire. He had grown taller since I had last seen him; he looked prettier and in better health too.

'This is Linton,' said Heathcliff. 'Don't you remember your cousin, young lady?'

'What, Linton?' cried Catherine in surprise. Linton walked forward and greeted his cousin. Catherine too had grown taller. She was a beautiful young woman; her whole being was sparkling[2] with life. In contrast, her cousin looked pale and apathetic, but he did not seem as bad as I remembered him.

'So you are my uncle, then?' said Catherine, reaching up to kiss Heathcliff.

He pushed her away. 'If you have any kisses to spare, give them to Linton. They are wasted on me.'

'Why do you never visit us?' Catherine asked Heathcliff.

'Because your father and I do not speak to each other. Your father

---

1. **revenge:** 報復、報仇   2. **sparkling:** 閃爍的，這裏指充滿活力

thought I was too poor to marry his sister. If you want to see your cousin again, you must not tell your father you have been here. He dislikes me so much that he would not let you come here.'

'Then he is wrong,' said Catherine, 'I shall ask him to let Linton come and visit us at the Grange.'

'The journey would kill me,' said Linton quietly, 'It would be better if you came here, Miss Linton, once or twice a week.'

Heathcliff looked at his son with contempt[1]. Then he turned to me and said, 'I am afraid Miss Catherine will see what a pathetic creature my son is, then she will send him to the devil and refuse to marry him. I am sure he will die before he even reaches eighteen. If only he were Hareton. I would have loved Hareton if he had not been Hindley's son, but I do not think the girl will fall in love with *him*. Look at Linton, Nelly, he is more concerned[2] with drying his feet than paying attention to his cousin.' Turning to Linton, he said out loud.

'Have you nothing to show the young lady, here? A rabbit's nest? Take her into the garden before you take off your shoes.'

'Wouldn't you rather stay here?' Linton, asked Catherine as he sat down by the fire.

'I don't know,' she said, but looked towards the door, and I knew she was eager to get out into the fresh air and explore.

Heathcliff went out and called to Hareton. The two came back, and I saw that Hareton had washed his face and combed his hair.

'That's not my cousin, is it?' Catherine asked Heathcliff.

'It is,' he answered, 'the son of your mother's brother. He's a handsome young man, isn't he?'

Catherine stood up on tiptoe[3] and whispered something in Heathcliff's ear, making him laugh. Hareton's face darkened.

---

1. contempt: 蔑視
2. concerned: 關注

3. on tiptoe: 踮着腳尖

'Now Hareton, you take her round the farm. And behave like a gentleman, no bad language, and don't stare. Keep your hands out of your pockets. Go now, and entertain her as nicely as you can.'

Heathcliff laughed an evil laugh as he saw them go. 'Hindley would be proud of his son, Nelly, don't you think?' He spoke to Linton then, 'If you don't want someone else to take your cousin from you, get up now and follow them, you lazy boy.'

Linton got up weakly from his chair, and as he joined Hareton and Catherine, I heard her ask Hareton about the carving above the door.

'I don't know what it is. It is some writing. I cannot read it,' he said crossly.

'Can't read it?' she exclaimed in surprise.

Linton laughed. 'He cannot read,' he said to Catherine. 'Have you ever met a bigger dunce[1]?'

'Well, he does seem stupid at times,' she laughed, looking at Hareton.

Linton went on to describe how stupid and ignorant their cousin was, while Hareton's face burnt with shame. I began to dislike Linton more than feel sorry for him. I could understand why his father did not think much of him.

On our way home that afternoon, Catherine told me how excited she was to meet her cousin and her uncle, and that her father was wrong to dislike them, and she would tell him so.

Fortunately, she did not see her father that day, and I waited anxiously to see what would happen when she spoke to him the next day. ◼

---

1. **dunce:** 遲鈍的人、蠢人

Reading Comprehension

1 **Choose the best answer – A, B, C or D.**

1 Why does Edgar decide not to tell Catherine where Linton has gone?

A ☐ He doesn't like Linton and does not want them to be friends.

B ☐ He wants to punish Heathcliff.

C ☐ He thinks that Catherine will run away.

D ☐ He does not want Catherine to come into contact with Heathcliff.

2 What does Heathcliff think when he meets his son for the first time?

A ☐ He thinks his health will improve at Wuthering Heights.

B ☐ He is pleased to have someone to help with the farm work.

C ☐ He is disappointed and thinks Linton is pathetic.

D ☐ He is disappointed but hopes that he will become friends with Hareton.

3 How does Linton react when Nelly leaves him at Wuthering Heights?

A ☐ He waves to Nelly as she leaves.

B ☐ He cries at first, but cheers up when he is given some food.

C ☐ He is frightened of his father and does not want to stay.

D ☐ He makes her promise to come back the next day.

4 What does Heathcliff think of Hareton?

A ☐ He wants him to marry Catherine.

B ☐ He thinks that he needs a wash.

C ☐ He loves him because he is Hindley's son.

D ☐ He is sorry that Linton is his son and not Hareton.

5 How do Linton and Catherine treat Hareton?

A ☐ They ignore him besause he is only a farm worker.

B ☐ They laugh at him for not being able to read.

C ☐ They accept him as their cousin.

D ☐ They decide to help Hareton and teach him how to read.

FCE – Grammar

2 **What might have happened? Complete the following sentences using the past perfect and the correct hypothetical form.**

1 If Linton _____ so weak, then Heathcliff _____ him. *(not be, might love)*

2 If Heathcliff _____ his son, both of them _____ happier. *(love, be)*

3 If Edgar and Heathcliff _____ each other, then Catherine and Linton _____ friends. *(not hate, could be)*

4 If Catherine _____ so disobedient, she _____ Linton again. *(not be, never see)*

5 If Hareton _____ to read, Catherine _____ at him. *(be taught, not laugh)*

6 If Linton _____ nicer, Nelly _____ sorry for him. *(be, would feel)*

FCE – Writing

3 **Catherine now knows both her cousins. Finish her diary entry where she describes them both. Write 120-150 words.**

Monday, 5th November 1800

Dear Diary,
Hareton and Linton are so different from each other that I cannot believe they are both my cousins!

Vocabulary

4 Find the correct word from the definitions below, then complete the crossword.

Clues

Across

2 bubbly, vivacious
5 in a panic
6 thick liquid food made from oats and milk or water
7 extremely surprised
12 convince
13 precious/valuable things
14 something that you own
16 shaking

Down

1 mistake
3 power over somebody or something
4 what you feel if you think someone is worthless
8 compassion
9 curious
10 small, evergreen plant, with purple flowers
11 when you travel, you go on a...
15 opposite of right

Speaking

5 **Do you agree or disagree with the following statements? Discuss in pairs and give reasons for your answers.**

	Agree	Disagree
1 Edgar was right not to tell Catherine where Linton had gone.	☐	☐
2 Edgar was right to let Linton go to Wuthering Heights.	☐	☐
3 Linton was right to be frightened of his father.	☐	☐
4 Heathcliff was right to be disappointed in Linton.	☐	☐
5 Catherine and Linton were right to humiliate Hareton.	☐	☐

PRE-READING ACTIVITY

6 **Before you read Chapter Eight, decide if the following statements are true (T) or false (F).**

	T	F
1 Edgar does not want Catherine to enjoy being with her cousin Linton.	☐	☐
2 Edgar says Heathcliff enjoys destroying people he hates.	☐	☐
3 Catherine thinks her father is wrong not to let her see Linton.	☐	☐
4 Catherine and Linton start writing secret love letters to each other.	☐	☐
5 Nelly finds the letters and makes Catherine burn them.	☐	☐
6 Nelly shows the letters to Catherine's father.	☐	☐
7 Nelly does not believe that Linton is dying because of Catherine.	☐	☐
8 Catherine and Nelly tell Edgar they are going to Wuthering Heights.	☐	☐
9 Catherine does not believe that Linton is ill.	☐	☐
10 Hareton kills Linton.	☐	☐

Chapter Eight

'Linton is dying, because you have broken his heart.'

9 The next day Catherine told her father all about the visit. I hoped that he would tell her honestly why he did not want her to visit Wuthering Heights, but it was not in his character to be open in that way. The reasons he gave for his dislike of the people at Wuthering Heights were not convincing[1].

'Do you know why I did not want you to see Linton?' he asked his daughter, pulling her towards him. 'Did you think it was because I did not want you to enjoy being with your cousin?'

'It was because you dislike Mr Heathcliff,' she answered.

'Then you think I care more about my feelings than I do about yours. No, it is because Mr Heathcliff does not like me. He is a most diabolical man. He enjoys destroying the people he hates, and I knew that if you kept seeing your cousin, then it would bring you into contact with him. I knew that he would detest you because you are my daughter. I should have told you all this before. I am sorry I have waited so long.'

'But Mr Heathcliff seemed very welcoming, papa. He does not mind if Linton and I see each other. He said you quarrelled[2] because he married Aunt Isabella, and you won't forgive him. So you are the

---

1. **convincing:** 有説服力

2. **quarrelled:** 爭吵

one to be blamed. He is happy for Linton and I to be friends, and you are not.'

Edgar understood that he had no choice but to tell Catherine much more about what had happened all those years ago. He gave her a short account of how Heathcliff had treated her aunt and finished by saying.

'She would have been alive today, if it had not been for him!'

Catherine had led such a gentle life, protected from all that was bad, that she was very shocked that anyone could be so wicked. Edgar ended the conversation, saying they would talk about it another day, and that she was to return to her studies. She obeyed him and sat quietly studying her books, but when I went to help her get ready for bed that evening, I saw that she had been crying.

'I'm not crying for myself, Nelly. It's for Linton. He expected me to come and see him tomorrow, and he will be disappointed.'

'Don't be so silly[1],' I said to her crossly. 'He has spent all these years not seeing you. He will not mind not seeing a cousin he has only met twice in his life.'

'But can't I write him a note? Can't I send him the books I promised him?'

And when I said no, and that her father had clearly said to her she must not see him or write to him, and that I would make sure his orders were obeyed[2], she gave me such a naughty look that I did not want to kiss her goodnight. I left the room and shut the door, but before I had gone a few steps, I changed my mind. I felt sorry for not kissing her. When I opened the door, what did I find? That naughty little miss was standing with a pencil in her hand and a note on her desk which she tried to hide from me as I came in.

---

1. silly: 愚蠢的、傻的   **2. obeyed:** 遵從

'You won't find anyone to deliver that for you,' I said, and without waiting to hear her protests, I put out her candle and told her to get straight to bed.

It wasn't until some weeks later that I discovered the note had been taken to Linton by the boy who delivered milk, and that many notes had passed between Catherine and Linton in this way.

It was when I was tidying her things one day, that I found a pile of love letters hidden in a drawer in her desk. I told her I would put them in the fire and that she was to stop writing to her cousin. She argued and fought, but then I said I would take them to her father to show him, and he would be very upset by her disobedience. Catherine loved her father and so, eventually, she agreed to me burning them. She watched sadly as the fire turned the paper to black ash[1], and the next morning I sent a note via the milk boy saying, 'Master[2] Heathcliff is requested to send no more notes to Miss Linton as she will not receive them.' I thought that was an end of the matter.

Summer passed into Autumn, and Catherine became quiet and sad. Her father decided she needed to spend more time outside, and they spent many afternoons walking in the fields, watching the harvest. Then Edgar got a bad cold and could not leave the house, so I went out with her instead; but I was a poor substitute for the father she loved so much. She walked slightly ahead of me, and when I caught up with her, I saw that she was crying.

'Catherine, why are you crying, love?' I asked. 'You mustn't cry because papa has a cold; be thankful it is nothing more serious.'

1. **ash:** 灰燼

2. **Master:** （舊時加在男孩的姓或者名字前的稱謂）小主人

'But I am so worried about papa. What will happen to me when you and papa are dead, and I am on my own?'

'Oh, your papa is still young, and I am strong and only forty-five.'

On hearing this her face brightened[1], and she began to run ahead of me as she had always done, and soon we came to a locked door in the wall that ran around the Park. Catherine climbed up to sit on top of the wall. She was trying to pick some berries[2] from a tree, when her hat fell off and landed on the ground on the other side of the wall. Catherine immediately jumped down to get it, but she could not climb back up. The wall on that side, by the road, was too smooth.

'Stay where you are,' I said. 'Maybe I have the right key to open the door.' I tried all the keys that I carried with me as housekeeper, but none of them would open the door.

Suddenly, Catherine whispered to me anxiously.

'I wish you could open the door, Nelly.'

Then I heard a horse arriving, and a deep, male voice said,

'Miss Linton, I am glad to meet you. I need you to tell me something.'

'I will not speak to you, Mr Heathcliff,' Catherine answered. 'Papa says you are a wicked man, and you hate both him and me, and Nelly says the same.'

'I'm not interested in what they say,' said Heathcliff. 'I don't hate my son, and it is him I wish to talk to you about. Yes! You have good reason to blush, Miss Linton. Two or three months ago, you were in the habit of writing little love letters to Linton, weren't you? I have your letters, and if you give me any trouble, I will take great pleasure in sending them to your father.

I suppose you became bored with Linton and decided to drop him.

---

1. brightened: 令人快活起來　　　　**2. berries:** 漿果

Well, you have hurt Linton deeply. He really was in love with you, and now he is dying because you have broken his heart. He will be dead before next summer, and it will be your fault.'

'How can you tell such terrible lies to the poor child?' I cried from the other side of the wall. 'Miss Catherine, do not listen to such nonsense.'

'I did not realise that there were eavesdroppers[1],' he muttered. 'How can you tell the 'poor child' such terrible lies about me?' Then, speaking to Catherine, he said, 'I will be away from home all week. If Nelly won't let you go to Linton, then you come by yourself. If I am not at home, then your father will not mind you visiting your cousin.'

I picked up a stone and used it to break the lock on the door. Catherine was looking up at Heathcliff, but she did not see his deceit[2] – it was hidden behind eyes filled with apparent concern for his son.

'Miss Linton,' Heathcliff continued. 'I admit I have little patience with my son, and Hareton and Joseph have even less. I think it may be your kindness as much as your love that he misses. He dreams of you night and day, and thinks that you hate him, because you do not write to him or come to see him.'

I pulled Catherine through the door and shut it firmly and we went straight back to the house.

That evening Catherine was terribly sad – she had been worried about her father, now she was also worried about her cousin. Heathcliff had been devilishly clever. Nothing I said could stop her believing that every word that man said was true.

The next day, I made a decision. Since Heathcliff was away and

---

1. **eavesdroppers:** 偷聽者、竊聽者   2. **deceit:** 欺騙

her father ill in bed, Catherine and I would go secretly to Wuthering Heights, and then she would be able to see with her own eyes that Linton was not dying.

It was a cold damp October day when we set out, and by the time we entered the kitchen, where Joseph was sitting next to a large fire smoking his pipe, my feet were completely soaked, and I was in a bad mood.

As Catherine ran to warm herself by the fire, we heard a cross, whining voice from the other room.

'Joseph, how many times do I have to call you? Come and put more coal[1] on my fire at once!'

When the old man did not answer him, he continued, 'I hope you starve[2] to death and die all alone!'

Joseph did not get up, so Catherine went in to Linton and threw her arms round him. He pushed her away weakly, hardly able to lift his head from his chair.

'No, don't kiss me. It takes my breath. Father said you would call.' He stopped, apparently without breath to speak. 'Will you shut the door?' he asked, 'That detestable old man will not bring coals to the fire, and it is so cold.'

'Well, Linton,' said Catherine. 'Are you pleased to see me?'

'Why didn't you come before?' he answered. 'You should have come instead of only sending letters. Writing made me tired. I would rather have talked to you and now, I am too tired to write or talk. Get me a drink,' he said, turning to me. I was not happy to be spoken to in that way, so it was Catherine who went to get him some water. When she came back, he said, 'Papa told me you hated me, and that was why you would not come.'

1. coal: 煤   2. starve: 挨饿 ▶FCE◀

'Oh, Linton, next to Papa and Nelly, I love you more than anyone. It is Mr Heathcliff I do not like.'

'He is often out during the day,' Linton said. 'so, you could come and see me, couldn't you? You would make me better.'

'If only Papa would let me,' said Catherine, stroking Linton's long blond hair, 'I would spend half my time with you. I wish you were my brother.'

'Papa says you would love me better than anyone in the world if you were my wife. I would rather you were my wife than my sister,' he said.

'But people sometimes hate their wives, but never their brothers and sisters.' Catherine said. 'Your father hated your mother.'

I tried to get her to stop, but she carried on until she had said everything she knew about Linton's mother and father. Linton did not believe her.

'Well, your father must have been wicked for Aunt Isabella to leave him,' Catherine said.

'She didn't leave him!' said Linton.

'She did,' continued Catherine.

'Well, I will tell you something,' said Linton angrily, 'Your mother hated your father – she was in love with mine!'

'You little liar,' she said, furiously.

'She was, she was,' he sang, triumphantly[1]. Catherine was so angry that she pushed him back in his chair. Linton began to cough[2]. He coughed for so long and so violently we became very worried. I held his head, while Catherine stroked his hair, until the boy was calm, and they had forgotten their argument.

Linton said she was the only one who could make him better, and

---

1. triumphantly: 得意洋洋地　　　　**2. cough:** 咳嗽

that she must come back and see him. I said that would not happen, but as we were leaving, she whispered something in his ear which made him smile.

That evening I came down with a cold, and I was so poorly that I had to stay in bed for three weeks. Catherine looked after both her father and me in the morning and then again in the evening. I did not think how she spent the rest of the day.

One day, at the end of the three weeks, I began to feel better and left my room. I saw that Catherine seemed anxious, so I asked her what was the matter. To my surprise, she burst into tears.

'Please promise you will not be angry,' she said. 'But since you have been ill, I have been to see Linton, and he is so much better. Sometimes he is cross, but we soon become friends again. We have spent so many lovely hours together. One time,' she continued, 'I thought how nice it would be to play a game. I opened a cupboard and found two balls under a pile of other toys. One was marked with 'C' and the other with an 'H'. I took the one with 'C' because I am Catherine, and I gave him the one with 'H', since his family name is Heathcliff. Later, I saw Hareton and he said, 'Miss Catherine, I can read those words above the door now,' and he read the words 'Hareton Earnshaw' in such a slow and stupid way that I laughed at him.'

'Oh, you should not have laughed at him,' I said, feeling sorry for Hareton. 'He was trying to please you.'

Catherine shook her head. 'Hareton came in later, in a violent rage[1], took Linton by the arm and shouted, "Go to your room! Take her there if she comes to see you!" And he picked Linton up and carried him up the stairs. Linton went completely white, and he

---

1. **rage:** 盛怒

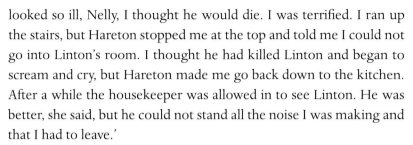

looked so ill, Nelly, I thought he would die. I was terrified. I ran up the stairs, but Hareton stopped me at the top and told me I could not go into Linton's room. I thought he had killed Linton and began to scream and cry, but Hareton made me go back down to the kitchen. After a while the housekeeper was allowed in to see Linton. He was better, she said, but he could not stand all the noise I was making and that I had to leave.'

'I sobbed and wept, while Hareton, who you seem to have such sympathy with, just stood there, telling me to be quiet and saying it was not his fault! I told him that I would tell Papa what had happened and that he would be put in prison and hanged[1]. Then Hareton began to cry and he left. I got on my pony, but Hareton was standing waiting for me by the gate.'

'"Miss Catherine," he started to say, and he did have a sorry look on his face. But I hit him with my whip[2] and rode straight home.'

As she spoke, I thought I had understood the reason behind Hareton's behaviour, but I did not say what I thought to Catherine.

After that, and in spite of her terror of Hareton, Catherine had gone back to Wuthering Heights. Her cousin had not been killed, but she was so worried about what Hareton might do to him, that she had continued to visit Linton, breaking her promise to her father.

When I told Edgar later what had happened, he was terribly worried. He told Catherine she must never go to Wuthering Heights again, however he did agree to Linton visiting them at the Grange. If Edgar had known how ill his nephew was and what a weak, unpleasant person he had become, I think he would not even have agreed to that.

1. hanged: 被絞死　　　　　　　　2. whip: 皮鞭

Reading Comprehension

1 **Answer these questions about Chapter 8.**

   1 What did Edgar say about Heathcliff?

   2 Why was Catherine so shocked when Edgar told her about Heathcliff?

   3 What was Catherine doing when Nelly went back into her room?

   4 What did Heathcliff say to Catherine to make her go back to Wuthering Heights?

   5 How was Linton when they arrived?

   6 What terrible secret did Catherine reveal to Linton?

   7 What terrible secret did Linton reveal to Catherine?

   8 Why was Hareton so furious?

   9 What did Hareton do to try to apologise?

   10 What did Edgar agree to let Catherine do?

FCE – Grammar

2 **Match the beginning and end of each sentence, then use the correct connecting word to join the two parts together.**

1 ☐ I knew that if you kept seeing your cousin, ...
2 ☐ I knew that he would detest you...
3 ☐ Her father had clearly said to her she must not see him...
4 ☐ I began to feel better...
5 ☐ He did have a sorry look on his face, ...
6 ☐ He told Catherine she must never go to Wuthering Heights again, ...

a _____ left my room.
b _____ you are *my* daughter.
c _____ he did agree to Linton visiting them at the Grange.
d _____ I hit him with my whip.
e _____ write to him.
f _____ it would bring you into contact with him.

3 **Time words. Use the time words and phrases in the box below to complete the following sentences.**

> After a while • That evening • The next day • long • until • now

1 I am sorry I have waited so _____.
2 It wasn't _____ some weeks later that I discovered the note had been taken to Linton.
3 _____ Catherine was terribly sad.
4 She had been worried about her father, _____ she was also worried about her cousin.
5 _____ I made a decision.
6 _____ the housekeeper was allowed in to see Linton.

Vocabulary

4 Circle the odd one out.

1	say	scream	shriek	shout	snap
2	cry	sob	weep	whine	whisper
3	bring	carry	drop	hold	take
4	cross	ill	pale	poorly	weak
5	angry	hang	hit	rage	violent
6	cupboard	door	room	shelf	table

_____ _____

_____ _____

_____ _____

_____

5 Eight words in the following extract have been replaced. Find the incorrect words then correct them.

I sobbed and smiled, while Hareton, who you seem to have such sympathy with, just danced there, telling me to be noisy and saying it was not his horse! I told him that I would tell Papa what had happened and that he would be put in prison and released. Then Hareton began to cry and he left.

I got on my pony, but Hareton was standing waiting for me by the moor.

'Miss Catherine,' he started to say, and he did have a cross look on his face, but I punched him with my whip and rode straight home.

Incorrect	Correct

Speaking

6 In Chapter 8, the characters continue to make bad decisions or behave badly. What would you have done instead to improve the situation? Look back at Chapter 8 to find examples of bad behaviour and decisions, write some notes in the box below, then discuss your ideas in pairs.

PRE-READING ACTIVITIES

7a What do you think is going to happen next? Before you listen to the last chapter, tick the events you think will happen.

1 Edgar's health gets worse. ☐
2 Edgar allows Catherine to see Linton. ☐
3 Linton is terrified: his father will kill him. ☐
4 Heathcliff keeps Nelly and Catherine prisoner at Wuthering Heights. ☐
5 Heathcliff forces Catherine to marry Linton. ☐
6 Catherine escapes, and her father dies in her arms. ☐
7 Linton dies. ☐
8 Heathcliff dies. ☐
9 Catherine teaches Hareton to read. ☐
10 Hareton and Catherine fall in love and decide to get married. ☐

▶ 10 **7b** Now listen and check your answers.

Chapter Nine

'The dead were now at peace.'

10 'These things happened last year, Mr Lockwood, and I can hardly believe what has happened since then.'

'Tell me more, Nelly. Did Catherine do what her father asked and stop going to Wuthering Heights?' I asked.

'She did. Her father was still the most important person in the world to her, and I am sorry to say that his health was getting worse – he had not recovered from that bad cold he had caught in the late autumn.'

Edgar called me one day and asked me to tell him truthfully what I thought about Linton.

'His health is very delicate, sir,' I replied, 'and I do not think he will live for many more years; but he is not like his father, a much weaker character. If Miss Catherine has the misfortune to marry him, she would be able to control him.'

Edgar sighed as I spoke.

'I have waited so long for my death to come.' He paused. 'I have been so happy with my little girl, Nelly. Through winter nights and summer days, she was a living hope at my side; but I have been as happy by myself at the church, up by Cathy's grave, longing[1] for

1. longing: 渴望

120

the time when I might lie there with her. What can I do for little Catherine? I would not mind that Linton is Heathcliff's son, I would not mind her marrying him, if he could console[1] her for my loss.

I would not even mind that Heathcliff would see their marriage as his greatest triumph. I would mind, however, if Linton is not worthy[2] of her, if he is a puppet[3] in the hands of Heathcliff. I cannot abandon Cathy to *him*!' I answered him as best I could. 'If we do lose you, sir, I will be her friend and counsellor to the end. She is a good girl. I do not believe she will deliberately choose to do what is wrong.'

The season turned to Spring and then to Summer, but Edgar's health did not improve. Catherine begged[4] and begged her father to let her see Linton, and eventually he agreed to her going with me, as long as he met us away from Wuthering Heights. When we got to the place we had arranged, however, Linton was not there. A messenger boy had been sent from Wuthering Heights to tell us he was a little further on. We found him lying in the heather very close to his home. He appeared so ill that Catherine looked at him in astonishment and grief.

'Why, Master Heathcliff!' I exclaimed, 'You are not fit to be out.'

'No, I – am – better, – better,' he panted[5], hardly able to breathe. He had great difficulty in maintaining a conversation with Catherine, and she could not hide her disappointment. Our company seemed more of a punishment than an enjoyment, so after only a short time, Catherine said we would be going. At that, Linton suddenly seemed to gain some energy; he looked fearfully back over to the house, asking her to stay another half hour at least.

'Please tell Uncle I am well,' Linton said, 'And if you see my father,

---

1. **console:** 安慰、安撫
2. **worthy:** 值得 ▶FCE◀
3. **puppet:** 傀儡
4. **begged:** 乞求
5. **panted:** 喘息

I beg you not to say to him that I have been extremely silent and stupid; don't look sad either.'

'I am not afraid of *him*,' said Catherine.

'But *I* am,' said Linton, shuddering.

Soon Linton's head dropped, and he stopped talking, only occasionally moaning from exhaustion or pain. We stayed with him, and when he woke again, he seemed terrified, asking if his father was coming. He was convinced that he had heard him. All we could hear was the wind.

We left, with Catherine promising to come back the next Thursday, but he seemed not to notice we had gone.

Over the next seven days, Edgar's health got much worse. Even Catherine began to lose hope that he would recover. She had just turned seventeen.

We waited until the Thursday afternoon to visit Linton. Edgar was in bed, and we did not want to disturb him, so we did not tell him we were going.

We met Linton lying in the heather in the same place near Wuthering Heights. This time he seemed more lively; I saw it was not joy that gave him this energy, but fear. Catherine became impatient with him.

'Catherine, don't look so angry,' he begged. 'I am a worthless coward, but save your hatred for my father.'

'What nonsense! Come Nelly, we are going home. Let go of my dress. Get up and don't behave like a snivelling[1] reptile[2].'

Linton began to cry in terror.

'Oh,' he sobbed, 'I cannot bear it! Catherine, I dare not tell you,

---

1. snivelling: 哭哭啼啼、抽噎　　　　**2. reptile:** 爬行動物

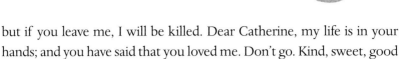

but if you leave me, I will be killed. Dear Catherine, my life is in your hands; and you have said that you loved me. Don't go. Kind, sweet, good Catherine. Perhaps you *will* agree, then he will let me die with you?'

'Agree to what?' said Catherine, her anger now replaced by concern.

'I cannot tell you. I dare not. My father threatened[1] me and I dread[2] him.'

She held him then as he sobbed. I watched them for a while, but then I heard footsteps, and I looked up and saw Heathcliff coming towards us.

'Get up, Linton! Get up!' he shouted. When he heard Heathcliff, Linton became helpless with fear. 'Now! Damn you.' Heathcliff repeated, and pulled his son to his feet.

'Stay with me, Catherine, give me your hand,' Linton said weakly.

'But Linton, I cannot go to Wuthering Heights with you. I am not allowed,' said Catherine.

'I can never re-enter that house,' he answered. 'I am not to re-enter it without you!'

He held onto her and repeated his request for her to accompany him. How could she refuse him? We did not know why he was so terrified, but neither of us could have left him on his own as he was.

When we got into the house, Heathcliff locked the door and said with a smile, 'There is no one here today but me. You must rest and eat.' Then he hit the table with his fist and, looking at Catherine and Linton, he said under his breath, 'How I hate those two.'

Catherine went towards Heathcliff, 'Give me that key,' she said, her black eyes filled with anger. 'I will have it. I wouldn't eat or drink here, if I were starving.'

Heathcliff pushed her back.

1. threatened: 威脅 ▶FCE◀　　　　　　**2. dread:** 害怕

'Now, Catherine Linton, stand back or I will have to knock you down.' Catherine was not afraid of him. She tried again to get the key, but her fingers were not strong enough, so she bit him. Heathcliff immediately raised his other hand to hit her, and he hit her, repeatedly, on the head. Seeing this diabolical violence against Catherine, I ran to stop him, but he pushed me over.

Visibly shaking, Linton told us why we were imprisoned at Wuthering Heights.

'Father wants us to be married, and he will not let you go until we are.'

Overcoming her fear, Catherine said, 'You must let me go to my father; he is dying. I will marry Linton, only you must let me go to him.' But Heathcliff did not let us go.

Later that evening, we learned that three servants from Thrushcross Grange had come looking for us, but they had been sent away by Heathcliff. We both started to cry uncontrollably, and Heathcliff locked us in an upstairs room.

At seven o'clock the next morning, Heathcliff came to get Catherine, but he kept me locked up. I knocked and banged at the door. Two or three hours passed before I heard footsteps outside my room. It was Hareton with a tray[1] of food for me, but he would not let me out that day, nor for the next five days.

On the afternoon of the fifth day, the housekeeper came in. She said the whole village thought that Catherine and I had got lost and died up on the marsh[2]. I pushed past her and went downstairs where I found Linton.

'Where's Catherine?' I asked.

1. **tray:** 托盤

2. **marsh:** 濕地

'She's upstairs. She must not go; we won't let her.'

'Won't let her? You little idiot!' I cried.

'I can't stand her crying, and she looks so pale and wild that I am afraid of her.'

I decided to leave that terrible house at once, and when I got back to the Grange, everyone was astonished and delighted to see me. They too thought I had died.

I went straight to tell Edgar what had happened. How he had changed in the five days since I had seen him. I did not think he would live another day! We sent four men to get Catherine, but the idiots came back without her – they had been told she was too ill to go with them. I planned to go back at dawn[1] to get her by force.

Later that night, with the harvest moon[2] shining in at the window, I heard footsteps coming into the house. Imagine my joy when I saw it was Catherine, though of course by that time she was Mrs Linton Heathcliff. Linton had eventually agreed to unlock her door so that she could escape.

Before she went up to her father, I warned her how ill her father was and that she must do everything in her power not to upset him. He had so little time left to live, and I did not want him to die worrying about his only daughter. I said she must tell her father that she was very happy to be Linton's wife so that he would die believing that all was well with her. She nodded her understanding, and later that night, he died peacefully in her arms.

The next events happened in quick succession. After the funeral, Heathcliff came to fetch Catherine, and now that he was my master, I was told to stay here at the Grange. A few weeks later, Linton's health became much worse. I found out afterwards that no one in the house

1. dawn: 黎明 ▶FCE◀   2. harvest moon: 滿月

had looked after the dying boy, except Catherine. She had stayed with him, watching her husband die for two weeks. Catherine begged for them to send for the doctor, but Heathcliff refused. He completely ignored his son's terrible suffering. Many months have passed since then, and still I have not seen Catherine, Mr Lockwood.

And so ended Nelly's story. I still had six months on my tenancy[1] at Thrushcross Grange, but I had grown tired of being in the country, so I decided to return to London early. I had been ill, and some time passed before I was well enough to go and say goodbye to my landlord[2]. When I got there, I did not stay long! Mr Heathcliff sat silent and grim, Hareton was absolutely dumb, and Catherine was sent to eat her meal with Joseph in the kitchen. I was not sorry to leave.

That was several months ago. Then, this September, I was visiting a friend in the north of England to go shooting with him. I saw I was not far from Thrushcross Grange, and I decided to go and see Nelly. When I got to the Grange, Nelly was nowhere to be seen, and I was greeted by a woman servant I had not met before. She told me, to my surprise, that Nelly was now working at Wuthering Heights. I went straight up to the old house.

'I have come to pay my rent,' I told her.

'You will have to talk to Mrs Heathcliff about that – this and the Grange belong to her now Heathcliff is dead.'

I was astonished. 'How did he die?' I asked, unable to believe that such a strong man could have died in such a short time.

'After you left, Heathcliff's behaviour became very strange. He

1. **tenancy:** 房屋土地的租賃期　　　　2. **landlord:** 房東

126

spent his nights out on the moors or by Cathy's grave. His anger and violence disappeared, and he stopped eating. Edgar, the man who had taken Cathy from him, was dead, and the revenge that had fed his dark heart no longer gave him any satisfaction.'

'One day, he told me that he had lost his appetite for violence. He became very distant, hardly noticing anyone or anything around him. When we did see him, he did not look at or talk to anyone; but instead, he looked behind us, as if there was someone else in the room who we could not see. Strangest of all, for someone I had never seen smile unless in cruelty, he always had a smile on his face.'

'One morning, I went into his room and saw that he had died in the night. I honestly think he had simply decided to die.'

'I am sure you will not believe the stories in the village, Mr Lockwood, but there are many people who say that they have seen Heathcliff and Cathy walking the moors at night. Once, I met a young boy looking after some sheep. He was crying and seemed terribly afraid. When I asked him what was the matter, he said he dare not take the sheep back down the road to the village because "Heathcliff and that woman were just down the road". Nothing I said could persuade him he was imagining things, and neither he nor the sheep would walk down the road.'

I shivered[1] in spite of the warm September sun. At that moment, Catherine and Hareton came running up to the house, hand in hand.

Hareton was dressed like a gentleman. He was completely transformed and Catherine was smiling with joy. I was amazed at how much they had changed.

'As Heathcliff began to withdraw from life, before he died, he began to leave them alone,' said Nelly, looking at the two young

---

1. **shivered:** 因寒冷或恐懼而顫抖 ▶FCE◀

lovers. He stopped shouting at them and threatening them. Catherine and Hareton began to spend more time together.

At first, she was as arrogant with him as she had always been, teasing him and laughing at his ignorance. How they argued! One day, when he was trying to teach himself to read, she mocked[1] him so much that he became furious with rage, threw the book he was reading on the fire and went out of the room. I don't know what happened to change her mind. Perhaps she was more relaxed now that Heathcliff was so distant or often out on the moors. But, whatever the reason, she stopped laughing at her cousin and, one day, she sat down next to him and patiently started teaching him to read. Hareton had always loved her, of course, but it took Catherine some time before she could see what a fine young man he really was under that rough[2] exterior. I am glad to say, though, that she did recognise Hareton's true value. I have never seen two people happier together. They are to be married next month, sir, and are going to live at the Grange.'

With the tyrant Heathcliff gone, it seemed to me, Catherine and Hareton were free to be themselves as they never had been before.

Before I left the next morning, I went to visit the graves of Edgar and Cathy. On the other side of Cathy, a woman I had never met, but whose story had filled my soul, there was a fresh grave and a simple stone marked 'Heathcliff'. I looked out over the moors and stood listening to the wind that blew gently in the trees. I did not believe that the dead walked the moors as ghosts. I was sure that they were at peace, leaving the living to find happiness at last.

1. **mocked:** 嘲笑   2. **rough:** 粗糙

Reading Comprehension

1 **Decide which of the following sentences refer to Heathcliff and Cathy (HC1) and which to Hareton and Catherine (HC2).**

		HC1	HC2
1	They loved each other from the beginning.	☐	☐
2	She did not like him at first and was embarrassed by him.	☐	☐
3	She laughed at his appearance.	☐	☐
4	She laughed at his ignorance.	☐	☐
5	She decided not to marry him because he was ignorant and dirty.	☐	☐
6	She decided to help him, taught him to read, and helped him become a gentleman.	☐	☐
7	They were passionate and wild.	☐	☐
8	They were joyful and content.	☐	☐

Grammar

2 **Put the correct word in the spaces below and say what types of words they are – the first has been done to help you.**

1 _____ (time word) I left the next morning, I went to visit the **2** _____ (_____) of Edgar and Cathy. On the other side of Cathy, a woman I had never met, but **3** _____ (_____) story had filled my soul, there was a **4** _____ (_____) grave and a **5** _____ (_____) stone marked 'Heathcliff'. I looked out **6** _____ (_____) the moors and stood listening to the wind that blew **7** _____ (_____) in the trees. I did not believe that the dead walked the moors as ghosts. I was sure that they were at peace, leaving the living to find **8** _____ (_____) at last.

Speaking

3 **Discuss the following questions in pairs.**

- Are you shocked by Heathcliff's behaviour in this chapter?
- What do you think of Heathcliff's treatment of Linton?
- What do you think of the young Catherine at the end of this story?
- Why do you think Heathcliff died?
- Are you pleased that this book has a happy ending?

Vocabulary

4 **Fill in the gaps in this famous poem by Amanda Crater. Use the words in the box below.**

> approval • condemn • encouragement • justice • love • ridicule • shame

If a child lives with criticism,
he learns to _____.
If a child lives with hostility,
he learns to fight.
If a child lives with _____,
he learns to be shy.
If a child lives with _____,
he learns to feel guilty.
If a child lives with tolerance,
he learns to be patient.
If a child lives with _____,
he learns confidence.
If a child lives with praise,
he learns to appreciate.
If a child lives with fairness,
he learns _____.
If a child lives with security,
he learns to have faith.
If a child lives with _____,
he learns to like himself.
If a child lives with acceptance and friendship,
He learns to find _____ in the world.

Speaking

5 **Now that you have read the poem, discuss the questions below in pairs.**

- Do you agree with the writer of this poem?
- Do you think that Heathcliff's childhood made him violent and vengeful, or was that part of his nature?
- Why do you think that Catherine and Hareton are so happy together? Do you think their childhoods were happier than Heathcliff and Cathy's?
- Do you think your childhood experiences can change you? Or do you think you are born with the character you have?

Emily Brontë (1818 - 1848)

Brontë sisters

Novelist and Poet

Emily Jane Brontë was an English novelist and poet. Although she is best remembered for her novel, *Wuthering Heights,* she was also a respected poet. She was born and lived most of her life in the northern English county of Yorkshire. It is a place of wild beauty which she loved. The character of the landscape she grew up in is mirrored in her writing, both prose and poetry. With her sisters Charlotte (*Jane Eyre*) and Anne (*Agnes Grey*), Emily was part of one of the most famous literary families in the world.

Early Life

Emily Brontë was born on 30th July 1818, in the village of Thornton, near Bradford, the fifth of six children. In 1824, her father was given the job of curate, or assistant vicar, at the nearby town of Haworth. The Parsonage at Haworth was where Emily lived for most of the rest of her life. From the beginning, Emily's life was filled with tragedy. Her mother died of cancer when she was three, then she lost her two oldest sisters – Maria who died at the age of 11 and Elizabeth who was 10.

Following an unhappy few months at a boarding school, Emily returned home and was educated there, along with Charlotte, Anne and her only brother, Branwell. One of her favourite activities was writing stories with her youngest sister Anne about imaginary worlds, including an island in the Pacific, called Gondal.

Brontë Parsonage Museum

Pseudonyms

Although Emily had brief periods away from home during her life, either to study or to work as a teacher, she was always longing to go home. When Charlotte discovered some of her poems, in the early 1840s, Emily was persuaded to get them published together with poems written by her two sisters. Because of the prejudice of the time against women writers – it was not thought appropriate for women to write – the three sisters decided to publish under the pseudonyms of Currer, Ellis and Acton Bell. The volume of poetry they published in 1846, was not a big success.

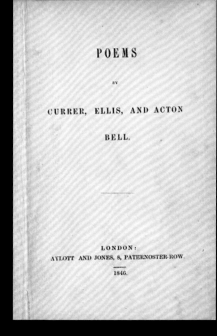

POEMS

BY

CURRER, ELLIS, AND ACTON

BELL.

LONDON:
AYLOTT AND JONES, 8, PATERNOSTER-ROW.
1846.

1846 issue of Brontë poems

Wuthering Heights

All three sisters began to work on novels after that. *Wuthering Heights* was published in 1847, under the name Ellis Bell. Contemporary critics immediately recognised the power and originality of the writing, but thought the book strange and ambiguous. Some critics were unhappy about the narrative structure of the book, with the story being told to us by Lockwood and Nelly Dean, and others were shocked by the amoral passion of its main characters, Cathy and Heathcliff. Since that time however, *Wuthering Heights* has been seen as one of the most important works of English literature.

Emily Dies

Following her brother Branwell's death in 1848, Emily caught a bad cold and died, probably of a severe chest infection, on 19th December 1848. She is buried in Haworth church. Anne Brontë died only a few months later. It was not until two years after her death, in 1850, that the only remaining Brontë sister, Charlotte, announced that she and her sisters were Currer, Ellis and Acton Bell. Many people could not believe that Emily, who had had such a quiet life, could have written a book of such power, violence and passion. They perhaps underestimated the power of her imagination.

Themes and Symbols

Love and Hatred

In the popular imagination, *Wuthering Heights* is about love and above all about the passionate love of Cathy and Heathcliff. However, the book is as much about hatred, cruelty and jealousy as it is about love, and the various types of love that are shown in the book are often destructive or unhealthy.

Cathy and Heathcliff

There are many different types of love in this novel. The most important type is the complex relationship between Cathy and Heathcliff. The love between Heathcliff and Cathy is as wild and uncivilised as the moors they grow up in. Cathy tells Nelly that she *is* Heathcliff, ' he is more myself than I am'.

Two strings to her bow, 1882

Cathy and Edgar

Cathy experiences two kinds of love. Cathy is happy with Edgar Linton, but she knows that her love for him is not the same as her love for Heathcliff and that it will change over time. "Whatever our souls are made, his and mine are the same, and Edgar's is as different as a moonbeam from lightning, or frost from fire." In the end, none of these three find permanent happiness.

Catherine and Hareton

The young Catherine also loves two men, but from the beginning we are told that her love is more gentle than her mother's. Her first husband is weak and ill. She appears to feel pity for him rather than love. When he dies, she falls in love with Hareton. Their love is joyful and tender – the opposite of Cathy and Heathcliff's ultimately destructive passion.

Children

Wuthering Heights also describes different types of relationships between parents and children. Some of these relationships are generally positive, most are not. Although the young Catherine is disobedient and her father, Edgar Linton, overprotective, she grows up happy and confident because she is loved and cared for. Her mother, Cathy, has a generally happy childhood, but by the end of his life, her father rejects her and her behaviour gets worse. As she grows up, she also sees a lot of physical violence, particularly from her brother Hindley. Heathcliff does not have any parents and is neglected and treated with violence and cruelty in his adopted family. Other children in this story also suffer. After his wife dies, Hindley ignores or bullies his son, Hareton, almost killing him in an accident when he is drunk. When Nelly is sent away from the house, Hareton becomes aggressive, is dirty and uses bad language. When Linton appears in the story, he is already ill and weak, however his treatment by his father is unforgiveable. Heathcliff threatens and bullies his son, until he is terrified of him. When Linton is dying, Heathcliff does not look after him or send for the doctor.

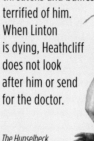

The Hunselbeck Children, 1806

Revenge

Through the course of the story, Heathcliff becomes increasingly obsessed with revenge. Everything he does is motivated by his desire to destroy everyone that he hates. Heathcliff starts with Hindley, who hit and humiliated him when he was a child. A strong insight into why Heathcliff is so obsessed by revenge comes after he has been severely beaten by Hindley. He sits by the fire in the kitchen, his head in his hands, and tells Nelly. "While I am thinking, I cannot feel the pain." He is using revenge to replace the pain and rejection he feels.

When Catherine chooses to marry Edgar Linton, Heathcliff has another motive for revenge. He hates Edgar for taking away 'his' Catherine. This need for revenge includes Isabella, whom he abuses simply because she is Edgar's sister, as well as his own son, Linton, and Catherine and Hareton, because of who their parents are. There is no logic behind this. Heathcliff's obsessive behaviour can therefore be seen as a form of madness.

Christmas comes but once a year, 1896

Class and Position in Society

In early nineteenth-century English society, your social class and position in society absolutely affected the kind of life you had. If you were from a poor family, you would get a job as a servant for a rich or middle class family from a very young age. Like Nelly, you would have spent your life looking after other people. In this society, there was no 'social mobility' – if you were born into a poor family, you could not move into a higher social class.

Heathcliff's class is one of the main themes in Wuthering Heights. Heathcliff is a foreigner and his family background is unknown, therefore he cannot be treated as an equal by the Earnshaws and the Lintons. Heathcliff resents this deeply. Cathy says she cannot marry Heathcliff because he is 'beneath' her socially, but by accepting the rules of her society, she goes against her nature. Heathcliff returns 'a gentleman' – he speaks and dresses well and is elegant, but for Edgar Linton he is still 'that farm boy, that foreigner.' What's more, these changes are soon shown to be superficial. He may look like a gentleman, but he is still as violent and aggressive as before.

It is left to Catherine Linton to overcome her social prejudices against Hareton, and by doing so she discovers love. Since Cathy's decision not to marry Heathcliff ends in tragedy, but her daughter follows her heart and finds happiness, it is likely that Emily Brontë was questioning the strict class rules of the society of the time.

Violence

On first reading this book, one of the most unexpected and shocking things the reader finds is the amount of physical and mental violence it contains. Almost everyone in the book is either the victim or the creator of violence. Heathcliff and Hindley, in particular, use violence as a way to control other people, destroying and threatening the people around them.

The supernatural

One of the most important and memorable scenes in the book is when Lockwood meets the ghost of Cathy on a wild, stormy night at Wuthering Heights. There is no doubt in his mind that the ghost is real. His fingers feel her ice-cold hand, he hears her voice and he even talks to her. On a number of occasions, it is suggested that Heathcliff and Cathy are possessed by a devil or a demon, and there are many references to heaven and hell. At the end of the story, Nelly tells Mr Lockwood that people in the village have seen the ghosts of Cathy and Heathcliff. She even met a terrified shepherd boy who had seen them – neither he nor his sheep would walk down that part of the road.

As if to reassure himself, and the reader, however, Mr Lockwood visits the graves of Cathy, Edgar and Heathcliff. It is a warm, sunny day in September. He says he does not believe that the dead walk – he is sure that they are now at peace.

Wuthering Heights and Thrushcross Grange

From the beginning we do not feel welcomed by *Wuthering Heights*. Its name, *Wuthering*, is a dialect word meaning wild and blown by storms. The house and its surroundings are as wild and uncivilised as the people who live in it – but they have their own strange beauty. In complete contrast is the aristocratic Thrushcross Grange, which represents the calm and order of the civilised world.

Task

Are the following sentences true (T) or false (F)?

	T	F
1 Emily Brontë was an orphan when she was three.	☐	☐
2 Her brother Branwell was also a famous novelist.	☐	☐
3 Emily was mostly educated at home.	☐	☐
4 Emily liked inventing stories from a young age.	☐	☐
5 At the time, it was not thought suitable for women to write.	☐	☐
6 Emily's pseudonym was Ellis Bell.	☐	☐

Adaptations

Wuthering Heights, 1939

On film

One of the best-known film versions of the novel was released in 1939 and starred Laurence Olivier and Merle Oberon. It is generally seen to be a great love story, but it is not an accurate version of the book – the characters and events are completely different from the novel. Like most of the adaptations, it cuts out the so-called second generation story, ie Catherine, Linton and Hareton. Timothy Dalton starred as Heathcliff in 1970. The film cuts out Catherine, Linton and Hareton, and it also leaves out Lockwood and the ghost of Cathy from the beginning of the book.
The 1992 version, starring Ralph Fiennes and Juliette Binoche, is a much more accurate adaptation. A model of the house of Wuthering Heights was built especially for the film, but it is not a farmhouse, more like a gothic horror castle.

TV

There have been a number of versions of the book made for TV, the best of these dates from 1998, starring Robert Cavanagh and Orla Brady. It is generally accurate and well acted.

Music

In 1978, singer Kate Bush released her first single, called *Wuthering Heights* – it went straight to number one and is still her biggest hit. This sinister song tells the story from Cathy's point of view, with some of the lyrics coming from the book ("Let me in! I'm so cold!"), and she talks about 'bad dreams in the night', as she calls for Heathcliff to join her in death – 'Let me have it, let me grab your soul away.'

Timeline of Events in *Wuthering Heights*

1500: The date above the entrance to Wuthering Heights

1757: Hindley Earnshaw born; Nelly Dean born

1762: Edgar Linton born

1765: Catherine Earnshaw born; Isabella Linton born

1771: Heathcliff brought to Wuthering Heights by Mr Earnshaw (late summer)

1774: Hindley sent to college

1777: Hindley marries Frances and comes back to Wuthering Heights when his father dies; Heathcliff and Cathy visit Thrushcross Grange, where Cathy stays for five weeks until Christmas

1778: Hareton born (June); Frances dies

1780: Heathcliff runs away from Wuthering Heights; Mr and Mrs Linton die

1783: Cathy marries Edgar; Heathcliff comes back

1784: Heathcliff marries Isabella; Cathy dies and Catherine born; Isabella runs away; Hindley dies; Linton born

1797: Isabella dies; Catherine Linton visits Wuthering Heights and meets Hareton; Edgar brings Linton back with him, but he is immediately taken to Wuthering Heights

1800: Catherine Linton meets Heathcliff and sees Linton again

1801: Catherine and Linton are married; Edgar dies; Linton dies a month later; Mr Lockwood goes to Thrushcross Grange and visits Wuthering Heights

1802: Mr Lockwood goes back to London; Heathcliff dies; Mr Lockwood comes back to Thrushcross Grange

1803: Catherine plans to marry Hareton

Family Tree

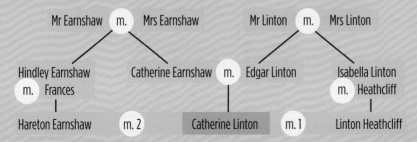

139

TEST YOURSELF 自測

1 **Answer these questions about the book.**

1 Who is living at Wuthering Heights when Mr Lockwood first visits the house?

2 Who is living at Wuthering Heights when Nelly goes to work there?

3 In which port did Mr Earnshaw find Heathcliff?

4 Which three servants are named in this story?

5 Apart from Thrushcross Grange and Wuthering Heights, one other building is mentioned in the story. What is it?

6 What is the name of the steep rocks behind Wuthering Heights where Catherine spends her first day with Hareton?

7 What forms of transport are mentioned in the story?

8 At the end of the story, how many people have died and what are their names?

2 **Who or what is being described in the following sentences?**

1 It is low and solid, made of dark stone, with a few short trees growing round it.

2 It is big and beautiful and has a large enclosed area of land around it called a park.

3 She has dark eyes and dark hair and has a wild, passionate nature.

4 He is tall, handsome, dark-skinned with dark eyes. He is passionate but he also is cruel, vindictive and violent.

5 He is weak, pale and ill and has a weak character.

SYLLABUS 語法重點和學習主題

//

Verbs:
Present perfect
Past perfect
Question forming and question
words
Irregular verbs
Would for willingness/refusal
Third conditional
If clauses (in zero conditional)
Used to and *would*
Phrasal verbs
Passive forms
Infinitive constructions

Conjunctions:
as, but, however, and, because

Determiners:
either, neither, none, both
little, some,
time phrases

Sentence types:
Relative clauses: embedded,
defining

Modal Verbs:
will
might
may
shall
could
should

Other;
Adverbs
Where clauses
Phrases with *when*
Time words

//

Wuthering Heights

Pages 6-7

1 1 d 2 c 3 g 4 h 5 b 6 e 7 a 8 f
2 1 c 2 e 3 a 4 g 5 b 6 h 7 d 8 f
3 1 is 2 is well named 3 to describe 4 roars
  5 did not grow 6 leant 7 to escape 8 heard 9 moaning
4 *Free speaking.*
5 *Free speaking.*

Pages 18-21

1 1 A 2 A 3 C 4 B 5 C 6 D
2 1 c 2 d 3 a 4 g 5 b 6 f 7 e
3a 1 snarled 2 shouted 3 laughed 4 talked 5 cried
  6 wailed 7 whispered 8 thundered 9 sobbed
3b **unhappy:** cry, sob, wail; **angry:** shout, snarl, thunder; **happy:** laugh; **speak normally:** talk, whisper
4a aggressive, desperate, repeatedly, sharply, suspiciously, unpleasantly, rude, vicious
4b 1 suspiciously 2 viciously 3 unpleasantly 4 aggressively 5 rudely 6 sharply 7 repeatedly
  8 desperately
5 1 up 2 on 3 from 4 by 5 at 6 as 7 into 8 as
6a 1 F 2 T 3 F 4 T 5 F 6 F 7 T 8 T
6b 1 Mr Lockwood returns home in the morning. 3 The housekeeper comes in with the tea.
  5 Mr Heathcliff doesn't live at Thrushcross Grange because he is very mean about money.
  6 Catherine is married to Heathcliff's son.

Pages 32-35

1 1 He heard Heathcliff's story from his housekeeper, Nelly Dean.
  2 He was found in Liverpool, and was probably foreign, but we do not know where he came from.
  3 Mr Earnshaw brought Heathcliff home because he was starving and homeless.
  4 Heathcliff's relationship with Hindley was very bad. Hindley was jealous and often hit Heathcliff.
  5 Heathcliff and Cathy were best friends from the beginning. They used to spend all their time together on the moors.
  6 Heathcliff and Cathy wanted to see how the young Lintons spent their Sundays and to see if Edgar and Isabella were punished as much as they were.
  7 They saw Edgar and Isabella alone in a beautiful room. They were arguing about a pet dog.
  8 A dog had bitten her ankle while she and Heathcliff were trying to run away. She stayed there until it healed.
  9 Before she went away, Cathy had been wild and naughty. When she came back, she had turned into a young lady, with expensive clothes which she was careful not to get dirty.
2 *Free writing.*
3 *Free speaking.*
4a **Positive:** forgiving, patient, harmless
  Negative: cross, depressed, dirty, disagreeable, horrible, mean,
    naughty, poisonous, silly, unkind, wicked, wild
4b **Joseph:** horrible, poisonous
  Frances: harmless, silly
  Hindley and Nelly: unkind
  Heathcliff: cross, dirty, disagreeable, forgiving, mean, patient, wicked
  Cathy: naughty, wild
  Mr Lockwood: depressed
5 1 feeling, doing 2 came 3 decided 4 have you been working 5 working
  6 was looking after 7 hated 8 being treated 9 gave 10 am planning
6 blow up, caught up in, came in, feed to, grew up, keep to, kept on, laughed at, live with, run away, sat

down, sent out of, stay out, tired of
7 *Free speaking.*
8b **1** T   **2** T   **3** T   **4** T   **5** F   **6** F   **7** F   **8** F   **9** F   **10** T

Pages 46-49
1 **1** HA   **2** F   **3** HI   **4** E-HI   **5** E-C   **6** C-E   **7** HC   **8** HC-C   **9** HC-HA   **10** E-C   **11** C-N-HC   **12** HC
2 **1** F   **2** T   **3** F   **4** T   **5** T   **6** F   **7** F   **8** T   **9** F   **10** T
3 *Free writing.*
4 **1** miseries   **2** miseries   **3** beginning   **4** love   **5** below   **6** always, always   **7** be separated
5 **1** should   **2** should   **3** must   **4** might   **5** would   **6** could
6 **1** D   **2** C   **3** D   **4** A   **5** B
7a I have dreamt in my life, dreams that have stayed with me ever after, and changed my ideas;
they've gone through me like wine through water and altered the colour of my mind.
7b *Free writing.*
8a *Free writing.*

Pages 60 to 63
1 **1** D   **2** C   **3** A   **4** B   **5** A   **6** C
2 **Heathcliff as a boy:** cursed, devil, patient, punished, neglected, rage, ragged, revenge, scowling, sulking, wicked
Heathcliff as a man: dignified, distinguished, fierce, gentleman, handsome, pitiless, tall, wolfish
Hidden name: Catherine Earnshaw
3 *Free writing.*
4a **1** He told me to tell him to come up.
   2 He eventually told him to sit down.
   3 She told me she could not rest.
   4 Cathy asked Isabella what she meant.
   5 I looked out of the window and told Heathcliff he had to go.
4b **1** 'Are they at home?' he asked.
   2 'Who is it, Nelly?' she asked.
   3 'Mr Hindley invited me,' he told her.
   4 'I love Heathcliff more than Cathy ever loved Edgar,' Isabella said.
5 *Free writing.*
6b stubborn, silent, tears, shocked, exaggerating, mad, bury, horses' feet, disowned, child, unhappy, fool, torture, confused, died

Pages 74 to 77
1 **1** C   **2** J   **3** D   **4** A   **5** G   **6** F   **7** K   **8** B   **9** E   **10** I   **11** H
2 **1** Isabella doesn't know how ill Cathy is. (Nelly believes that she would not have run away if she had known.)   **2** Edgar does look after Cathy and is patient with her. (Nelly says no mother could have looked after her child more patiently.)   **3** Isabella does care that she has upset her brother.   **4** Isabella has been unhappy at Wuthering Heights since she got there.   **5** Isabella is not free to leave Wuthering Heights. (She says she tried to once, but does not dare to again.)   **6** Cathy does not recognise Edgar before she dies. (Nelly says she did not regain enough consciousness to recognise Edgar or miss Heathcliff.)
3 Paragraph 1: **1** managed   **2** relief   **3** calm   **4** recover   **5** better
Paragraph 2: **1** ill   **2** upset   **3** terrible   **4** horrible   **5** filthy   **6** swears   **7** curses
4 *Free speaking.*
5 *Free writing.*
6a **1** 'Mr Linton does not worry about me.'
   2 'Nelly, will you tell him immediately how serious the situation is?'

3 'You do not love me any more.'
4 'I will/shall send someone after them.'
5 'Will you go to your room, woman?'
6 'Shall I come and see her again tomorrow?'
6b *Free writing.*
7 **1** gave - came - had eaten **2** remembered - had said **3** came - had managed
 4 understood - had happened **5** had seen - was
8 *Free speaking.*
9a *Free writing.*

Pages 88 to 91
1 **1** Edgar. **2** In a coffin in a downstairs room. **3** A locket. **4** Heathcliff. **5** A lock of blond hair.
 6 Isabella Heathcliff. **7** Hindley Earnshaw. **8** Isabella Heathcliff. **9** Linton. **10** Wuthering Heights.
 11 Hareton Earnshaw. **12** He was her cousin. **13** Linton. **14** Heathcliff's servant Joseph.
2 **1** your **2** as **3** as **4** his **5** in **6** by **7** out **8** so **9** do **10** over
3a **1** announcing **2** told **3** return **4** arrival **5** would be living **6** was **7** return **8** meeting
3b **1** gerund **2** simple past **3** noun **4** noun **5** reported future continuous **6** simple past
 7 noun **8** gerund
4 **1** loveliest **2** beauty **3** lively **4** spirited **5** gentle **6** thoughtful **7** tender **8** spoilt
5 **1** Wuthering Heights **2** twenty **3** Penistone Crags **4** frighten **5** horse **6** dogs **7** cousin
 8 bark **9** calm **10** Fairy Cave
6 *Free speaking.*
7 *Free speaking.*
8b 1 - 2 – 4 - 6 - 8

Pages 102 to 105
1 **1** D **2** C **3** C **4** A **5** B
2 **1** hadn't been - might have loved **2** had loved - would have been **3** had not hated - could
 have been friends **4** hadn't been - would never have seen **5** had been taught - wouldn't have
 laughed **6** had been - would have felt
3 *Free writing.*
4

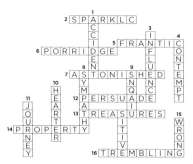

5 *Free speaking.*
6 **1** F **2** T **3** T **4** T **5** T **6** F **7** T **8** F **9** F **10** F

Pages 116 to 119

1 **1** He said that Heathcliff enjoyed destroying the people that he hated and that he would hate Catherine because she was his daughter. **2** Catherine had led a sheltered life, protected from anything bad, so she did not know that anyone could be so wicked. **3** She was secretly writing a note to Linton. **4** He told her Linton was dying of a broken heart and that he thought she hated him because she didn't go and see him any more. **5** Linton was in a bad mood, whining and complaining, and he seemed weak and ill. **6** She told Linton that his mother had left his father. **7** He told her that her mother had not loved her father, but had been in love with his father, Heathcliff. **8** Hareton was furious because Catherine and Linton made fun of him, and they didn't spend any time with him. **9** He waited for Catherine by the gate looking sorry. **10** He agreed to let Linton come to the Grange.

2 **1** f - then **2** b – because **3** e – or **4** a – and **5** d – but **6** c - however

3 **1** long **2** until **3** That evening **4** now **5** The next day **6** After a while

4 **1** say **2** whisper **3** drop **4** cross **5** hang **6** room

5 I sobbed and *wept*, while Hareton, who you seem to have such sympathy with, just *stood* there, telling me to be *quiet* and saying it was not his *fault*! I told him that I would tell Papa what had happened and that he would be put in prison and *hanged*. Then Hareton began to cry and he left. I got on my pony, but Hareton was standing waiting for me by the *gate*. 'Miss Catherine,' he started to say, and he did have a *sorry* look on his face, but I *hit* him with my whip and rode straight home.

6 *Free speaking.*

7b All of these events happen in Chapter Nine.

Pages 130 and 131

1 **1** HC1 **2** HC2 **3** HC1 **4** HC2 **5** HC1 **6** HC2 **7** HC1 **8** HC2

2 **1** Before (time word) **2** graves (noun) **3** whose (possessive pronoun) **4** fresh (adjective) **5** simple (adjective) **6** over (preposition) **7** gently (adverb) **8** happiness (noun)

3 *Free speaking.*

4 If a child lives with criticism, he learns to condemn.
If a child lives with hostility, he learns to fight.
If a child lives with ridicule, he learns to be shy.
If a child lives with shame, he learns to feel guilty.
If a child lives with tolerance, he learns to be patient.
If a child lives with encouragement, he learns confidence.
If a child lives with praise, he learns to appreciate.
If a child lives with fairness, he learns justice.
If a child lives with security, he learns to have faith.
If a child lives with approval, he learns to like himself.
If a child lives with acceptance and friendship, he learns to find love in the world.

5 *Free speaking*

Page 137

1 **1** F **2** F **3** T **4** T **5** T **6** T

Page 140

1 **1** Heathcliff, Hareton, Catherine, Joseph and Zillah. **2** Mr and Mrs Earnshaw, Cathy, Hindley and Joseph (and some other unnamed servants). **3** Liverpool. **4** Joseph, Nelly and Zillah. **5** The church. **6** Penistone Crags. **7** Horse and carriage. **8** Eleven people: Mr and Mrs Earnshaw, Mr and Mrs Linton, Edgar and Isabella Linton, Cathy and Hindley Earnshaw, Frances Earnshaw, Heathcliff and Linton.

2 **1** Wuthering Heights. **2** Thrushcross Grange. **3** Cathy. **4** Heathcliff. **5** Linton.

Read for Pleasure: *Wuthering Heights* 咆哮山莊

作　　者：Emily Brontë

改　　寫：Elizabeth Ferretti

繪　　畫：Gianluca Folì

照　　片：Getty Images, Marka

責任編輯：仇茵晴

封面設計：涂　慧　丁　意

出　　版：商務印書館（香港）有限公司
　　　　　香港筲箕灣耀興道 3 號東滙廣場 8 樓
　　　　　http://www.commercialpress.com.hk

發　　行：香港聯合書刊物流有限公司
　　　　　香港新界大埔汀麗路 36 號中華商務印刷大廈 3 字樓

印　　刷：中華商務彩色印刷有限公司
　　　　　香港新界大埔汀麗路 36 號中華商務印刷大廈 14 字樓

版　　次：2017年 9 月第 1 版第 1 次印刷
　　　　　© 2017 商務印書館（香港）有限公司
　　　　　ISBN 978 962 07 0472 7
　　　　　Printed in Hong Kong